PRAISE FOR A *CAGE OF ROOTS*

'Full of magic and mystery, deeply rooted in Irish mythology and legends ... this will keep you on the edge of your seat'
School Librarian Magazine

'An original and engaging fantasy, gorgeously, eerily illustrated by the author'
Children's Books Ireland Recommended Reading Guide

'A jam-packed adventure featuring time travel and Irish mythology'
LisaReadsBooks

'A gripping and truly frightening opening chapter ... Irish mythology is ingrained in Matt Griffin's novel and works to give it a depth that makes it stand out from other fantasy fiction'
booksforkeeps.co.uk

'Captivating ... an excellent midnight read for young goblins. The author is at his strongest while underground, depicting all the terrible and unimaginable horrors – a hellish dark place that suggests what would happen if Neil Gaiman and H.P. Lovecraft decided to co-write a gardening manual'
Inis

MATT GRIFFIN is from Kells, County Meath, and now lives in Ennis. He has garnered a reputation as one of the most eclectic graphic artists in contemporary illustration, collecting awards and accolades for his work in publishing, advertising and, in particular, the field of poster art. His passion for visual design was always married to one for writing. *A Cage of Roots* (2015) was his first novel for children.

MATT GRIFFIN

THE O'BRIEN PRESS
DUBLIN

First published 2016 by The O'Brien Press Ltd,
12 Terenure Road East,
Rathgar,
Dublin 6,
D06 HD27,
Ireland.
Tel: +353 1 4923333; Fax: +353 1 4922777
E-mail: books@obrien.ie
Website: www.obrien.ie
The O'Brien Press is a member of Publishing Ireland.

ISBN: 978-1-84717-783-4

10 9 8 7 6 5 4 3 2 1
21 20 19 18 17 16

Cover image: Matt Griffin

Printed and bound by CPI Group (UK) Ltd, Croydon, CR0 4YY.
The paper in this book is produced using pulp from managed forests

Published in:

DUBLIN
UNESCO
City of Literature

For my folks

ACKNOWLEDGEMENTS

Thanks to all at The O'Brien Press, especially Susan and Emma for helping me through the 'difficult second album'. Thanks to Orla for even more faith and patience. Thanks to my daughters, Holly and Chloe, for your constant inspiration. And finally, thanks to my family and friends for your unwavering support, as always.

The Land of
FAL

MUIRThEMNE

TARA

danann

Contents

When the Old Stones, faced with spiral line
Glow along those ancient scores
The Daughter wrenched back to her time
By blackened claws through ancient doors
The heroes felled, their promise failed
As dead as autumn leaves
Then all is lost, the wind will wail,
To the storms that she will weave.

Prologue

My uncles are gone.

Ayla's thoughts surged around the inside of her skull, tossed like a ship on a stormy ocean. The pain of mourning rose in huge mountainous waves and crashed against her, their violence so intense she felt as though she might drown under their weight.

They're gone. Just … gone! Disintegrated in front of me!

In all the terror she had faced in the last few days (had it been days? She couldn't tell) there had at least always been the hope that she would see them again; that they would once again save her and look after her and give her a happy life. There had been moments in the dark, stuffy cell, where she had been a prisoner of the Red Root King and his goblins, when she had contemplated just giving up. But in those moments she clung to the love of her uncles and her three best friends – Finny, Sean and Benvy – and the fear of never seeing them again gave her strength.

And now I'm risking the lives of my friends again.

There had been another feeling in the cell. One that she had never quite shaken despite all the tortures the goblins and their master had brought upon her. It was a sense of, of all things, *belonging*. Like the Ayla in those hellish tunnels was the *best* Ayla. A sense that if she was to be really, properly, true to herself it was down here, further from home than ever before and deeper into the dark.

And so even now, sick with loss, she pressed on through the choking dust into the blackness, hauling her three friends – the only family she had now – back into danger. And with every step she felt it was right. With every step she felt more powerful. With every step back into hell she felt more herself than ever.

CHAPTER 1

The Shattering Tunnels

S ean shut his dark eyes against the invading dust but it was no use. Even with the remains of his glasses for protection, the dust bit under his lids and his tears made seeing even harder. Every few minutes a distant boom sounded, the tunnel shook and fresh billows of grit filled the air. He realised then that they were all shouting, pleading with Ayla to slow down or anxiously calling out when their grip on each other's shirts slipped and for a few sickening moments they were alone in the chaos.

Confused and frightened in the dense fog of dirt, the group scrambled and crawled deeper into the void. Only a short time ago they had emerged from this accursed place, having risked their lives to save their friend. They had all skirted death by a whisker, none more so than Ayla herself. She had been a prisoner of things that only existed in horror films: a horde of goblins, minions of an entity called the Red Root King. He had tried to take her very soul in order to revive the life of his love: Queen Maeve. And Finny, Sean and Benvy had saved Ayla from his tortuous intentions only moments before the last ember of her life had been extinguished. Then they had all watched Lann, Fergus and Taig, the three giants of Kilnabracka and Ayla's beloved uncles, dissipate into the wind and sacrifice their lives for hers.

As she led her three friends back into the chaos of the goblin tunnels, Ayla's sadness was every bit as stifling as the dust. She ploughed through both with gritted teeth. Behind her, Sean, Benvy and Finny followed without question or protest, at least not vocally. They trusted her completely, and if she asked them to go back to the place that nearly killed them, she must have had good reason.

Silently, however, each of them struggled to think of a good reason why they weren't on the long way home by now. But the way Ayla's eyes had shone with dancing fronds of electricity made it quite clear that there was a lot more to her than they had realised and, as their friend, she should be trusted even if it meant going back into the pandemonium of the goblin tunnels. Whatever they were, they were loyal to her, no matter what.

For her part, Ayla's head was whirling. She felt as if she was divided into different people in the same body. Of all the things that had happened to her: waking up in a stuffy, dark pit and finding herself the prisoner of actual *goblins,* escaping into the tunnels only to get nearly eaten by a giant toad, and having her soul wrenched from her on the loom – the knowledge that she was the child of such malevolent beings was what shocked her most.

It's still just like a bad dream! How can those things be my parents? What does that make me?

Independently of her will, Ayla's legs and arms urged her deeper into the hell from which they had only just escaped; she simply charged on, unwavering in her mission to rescue the goblins and return them to their true forms. *They were girls once, just like me.* She had realised this because on that dreaded loom, she had nearly become one of them.

The sadness of losing her beloved uncles churned in her stomach, stirring up so much bile she thought it would come out in her tears. *They have just died. They have just died. They have just died.* The words ricocheted in her brain. *Lann, Fergus and Taig died for me. And I still don't know why?*

I don't know why any of this has happened. Please God, let me wake up.

But Ayla knew she was awake, and that this was real and it frightened her so much. Still she pushed on through the darkness, her tears carving wet tracks through the dirt on her cheeks.

Sean's hammer, Benvy's javelin and Finny's sword – magical weapons they had risked their lives to earn – gave off a faint blue light that was useless in the murky black tunnels, and cumbersome too. Sean, in particular, struggled to heave the great hammer through narrow gaps with only one hand while his other hand grasped for Benvy's shirt in front of him.

'Please, slow down!' he croaked, his mouth filling instantly with dust. But his pleading was lost in the chaos.

Sean's grip on Benvy's shirt slipped for the hundredth time, and his pack snagged on the low ceiling. He hollered for his friends to stop, and put every ounce of his strength into freeing his pack. He shut his eyes, clenched his teeth, pulled his pack from where it snagged and clawed at the earth to move himself along again, but their voices were fading, and then they were gone and he really was alone in the shuddering tunnel.

Panic squeezed at his stomach, wringing it out like a wet cloth. 'NO!' he shouted, but his desperate cry went unheard. Awkwardly, he wriggled himself into a position where he could reach the straps on his shoulders and remove his rucksack. Freed of that burden, he crawled along the shingly floor, hauling Fergus's huge hammer behind him. When he could raise his head again he pulled himself up into a crouch and shuffled. After a few metres he could stand almost to his full height. There was another deafening boom, and the aftershock flung him first against one wall and then the other. He rubbed his shoulders, coaxing movement back. Then he cleared his throat, picked up the hammer and pushed on through the veil of soil and sand to find his friends, sure that they were just ahead.

The dim glow of the hammer showed deep-hewn likenesses of gurning creatures on the walls. They were carved in complex mosaics of intertwining knots, like the old Celtic designs found on Irish souvenirs, except these ones featured wide-eyed monsters that chilled the blood. They were even more unsettling in the ghostly blue light. Sean tried not to look and concentrated instead on the floor and on keeping his footing on the loose gravel. He thought back to the day in Coleman's Woods, when Ayla had gone missing and they had all gone looking for her. He wished with all his heart that Benvy would play one of her tricks and jump out of the murk to frighten him. At every turn he prayed for it to happen, but it never did. He called after the others between coughing and half-choking with the dirt, until the shouting and invading dust made his throat too raw and hoarse. He pressed on with the hammer pushed out in front, until at last the walls widened, the ceiling rose enough for him to stand and the air cleared just enough to breathe a little easier. In the meek light, Sean could just about make out where he was. It was the first fork in the tunnel – the place where Finny had gone off alone in search of Ayla and ended up getting himself captured.

He remembered that the path he and Benvy had taken led to a dead end at the cell where they had found Ayla's phone. *Oh Benvy*, he thought, *please, please tell me you've remembered it too and you've gone the other way!* He tried to call out again, but his voice was only a rasp. Then Sean heard something: a shout, lost in the gloom. He tried frantically to call back but only a rasping sound came out. Then there it was again: a voice muffled by dust clouds but definitely a human voice. It was coming from the tunnel that branched off to the left. He didn't hesitate, and ran as best he could straight towards the noise, hauling the hammer behind him. Just past the mouth of the new corridor, he stepped into nothing but empty space, and fell a long, long way, the hammer clattering beneath him into the shadows.

Moments before this, Ayla, Benvy and Finny had suffered a similar fate. None of them had noticed the ground fall away beneath their feet and they too had fallen painfully into some deep crevasse. Benvy groaned and tried to stand. Her tailbone ached, having borne the brunt of the impact and she felt a trickle of blood course down her cheek. It was a big fall, but mercifully nothing was broken.

'Sean! Finny! Guys, are you okay? Is everyone okay? Ayla?'

'Ugh!' groaned Finny from the darkness. 'What happened? Ayla? You okay?'

'Yeah, I'm alright,' she answered. 'I think I came pretty close to being skewered by your sword, but I'm in one piece.'

'I think I'm okay too,' Finny replied. 'That hole wasn't there before. Anyone know where we are now?'

'Hang on,' Benvy interrupted. 'What about Sean? Sheridan! Where are you?'

But here was no reply. She tried again, now joined by the others.

'Sean! Are you there?'

Still there was no answer. They could see next to nothing, but groped around frantically to try and find their friend. The space was wider than the one they had come through, but strewn with rubble, the remnants of the collapsed floor above. At the other end the ground sank and then fell away entirely into a deep hole – the only way out. There was no sign of Sean. They shouted again, and this time the shout was answered by the sound of falling rocks. It came from behind one of the walls. Then there was a clatter of steel on stone, followed by a definite human yelp, and, at last, a dull thud.

'Here!' shouted Finny. He had found a gap in the wall about the size of a football. 'He's in there! I can see his hammer!'

Benvy shoved Finny aside. 'Sheridan? Sean? Are you alright?' she pleaded.

'Agggh!' came the strangled reply. 'I think I've broken … Wait! Benvy, is that you?'

'It's me!' she replied. 'It's us. We're all here. Are you hurt?'

'Oh, thank God!' Sean laughed, before wincing in pain. His voice was hoarse. 'I wasn't sure I'd ever find you. I got stuck and lost you guys a while back. I thought you knew.'

'We had no idea,' confessed Benvy. 'I thought you were just behind me. But are you okay? Is anything actually broken?'

'No I … I don't think so.' Sean groped around himself to make sure everything was in the right place. 'Just a bit battered. But how do I get in there?'

Benvy turned to the other two. 'We need to get him,' she said, and all three began looking for a way past the wall. There was none.

Finny put his face to the gap. 'Sean, is there any way out of there? Tell us what you see.'

Sean raised himself stiffly, located the hammer and held it out, using its faint blue light to see.

'It's mostly rubble. But hang on. There's a gap in the wall. Not your wall. The other one. It's tight but I can get through.'

'But how do we get there?' Benvy shouted. 'You need to get in here, not the opposite way, you eejit!'

Sean threw his eyes to heaven. 'I know that, Benvy. But I'm telling you there isn't a way. This is the only way out.'

'What about where you fell from?' Finny asked.

Sean pointed the hammer up to the ceiling.

'No,' he said, 'it's just a hole. No way up to it.'

'He's going to have to go his own way,' said Ayla. She surprised even herself with her lack of compassion, but it was clear to her that this was a delay they did not need.

Benvy and Finny turned to stare at her incredulously.

'What *are* you talking about?' Benvy asked angrily. 'He can't go off on his own. The whole place is collapsing! We need to stick together.'

Ayla felt a stirring of frustration, whipped into exasperation. She checked herself: *That's Sean! You need to get to him. What's the matter with you? This isn't you, Ayla! You're not that cold!* But from somewhere deep inside she felt anger broiling: *This is holding us back! We have to keep going!* It was as if there was another voice in her head. One that sounded like her, but wasn't Ayla at all.

'Look, Sean can't get in here, and we can't get in there. We're losing time. We have to press on! We're all going in roughly the same direction. He'll find us. But we have to get to Maeve *now*!'

At the last word, her eyes shone for a moment. She made for the hole in the far corner of their section of the tunnels.

'Ayla!' Finny shouted, trying in vain to reach out to his best friend.

Benvy couldn't believe they were even considering leaving Sean alone. She interrupted Finny, shouting out after Ayla, 'Hang on just one flipping second! That's our friend in there! And we're all back down here in this dis-integrating, evil, airless hell hole because of *you*! The least you can do is help keep us all together!'

Sean's voice made its way meekly though the gap in the tunnel wall. 'I don't want to be alone,' he murmured.

'There! You see?' Benvy was still shouting at Ayla's retreating back.

But Sean's voice went on, 'Ayla's right, though. The only thing you can do is keep going your way. I'll go through this gap, and hopefully we'll meet down the line.'

'What?' Benvy couldn't believe what she was hearing. 'Ah, Sean, would you stop trying to be a hero, for flip sake!'

'It's alright, Benvy. I'll meet you in a bit.' Sean reached a hand through the hole, and Benvy took hold of the tips of his fingers reluctantly.

'It's alright,' Sean said again, squeezing Benvy's hand as best he could. 'The tunnels probably join back up soon. I'll probably see you in five minutes.'

He took his hand away and Benvy could see him, in the faint light from his hammer, attempting a reassuring smile. Defeated and with a sinking heart, she said roughly, 'You'd bloody better, Sheridan. Then she turned to follow Finny and Ayla down through the hole.

They had just lowered themselves though the gap when there was a deafening bang behind them and the whole chamber they had just left shook violently, crumbling in a wreck of grinding stone and hissing dirt.

'Sean!' Benvy screamed, but there was no answer.

Finny, Ayla and Benvy found themselves clambering down a tight shaft, slipping on loose stone until it levelled and broadened into yet another chamber. Ayla wasted no time in searching for the next exit, while Finny tried to give Benvy a helping hand as she wriggled through to join them. She shrugged him off and hauled herself up.

'If anything has happened to Sean …' she started.

'He'll be fine, Benvy,' Ayla said, trying to hide her impatience. 'I know he'll be fine.'

'How the hell can you *know*?' Benvy shot back, frustration coursing through her voice.

'Benv',' Finny interjected diplomatically, 'it was only the room we were in that collapsed, I'm sure of it. Sean'll be okay, and as soon as we get a chance to split, I'll go looking for him, okay?'

There can be no going back, Ayla's mind was instructing her. *No separating. I may need all their help to get to her.*

Out loud, Ayla found herself snapping, 'No! We have to stay together now.' There was a slight pause, and Ayla's eyes flickered for a moment, and then, sounding more like herself, she said, 'Benvy, I love Sean too, you know, and I really hope he's not hurt. But we have to go on and let him make his own way. He's tougher than you think.'

As if that announcement solved everything, Ayla turned away from her friends and resumed her search for an exit.

Behind her Finny held up his sword up so that he could see Benvy in its cold light. He saw the worry etched on Benvy's dirty freckled face as she pushed her sandy-coloured hair out of her eyes. His own features mirrored hers.

'Finny, you need to try and talk to Ayla …'

'I know. I will. I'm not sure what's going on with her. She's just lost her uncles, Benvy. For now all we can do is keep on moving. We've got to find a way out of here,' he said.

They joined Ayla in exploring the space, running their hands along the walls and holding their weapons up for light. It was bigger than the last room, and the walls were coated in those horrible engravings.

'Here!' said Ayla. She had found a doorway, framed in the goblin motif. It was the first real doorway they had come to. 'We're heading in the right direction anyway. Watch out for hidden drops this time.'

Through the entrance they sensed a bigger space, with the warm, dust-deadened air able to circulate more freely. Immediately on the right, hanging on the wall, Finny found a blackened stick of wood. It stank of rotting meat.

'Urgh! These things reek!' he exclaimed.

'Wait, give it here!' said Ayla and reached out for it. She smelled it, and instantly recognised the stench. Bad memories of her imprisonment and the goblins' gruel came flooding back.

'Stand back!' she ordered. 'It's a torch. I'm not sure if this will work but …'

She stared intently at the stick, her forehead folded in concentration. *I can do things now*, she thought. *I feel power there, needling at my head.* It felt like a series of shocks, sharp and biting but somehow she revelled in them. She could feel something brewing behind her eyes, like a storm. It felt *good*.

Ayla held her gaze steady for what seemed like an age, and just as Benvy was about to ask what the hell was going on, Ayla's eyes lit once, twice, and then sparked into electric life. In a heartbeat, a flashing frond of electricity darted from her eyes and the wood took it hungrily. A blue flame danced on its tip, bright at first and then weak like a spent candle. It was more effective than the weapons, though, and Ayla asked the other two to get more blackened sticks from the walls.

'Take as many as you can carry,' she instructed. 'We'll need them.'

Finny and Benvy seemed hardly to hear what Ayla said. They were staring at her, finding it hard to believe this was the Ayla they knew.

Finally, Finny said something. 'Ayla, what the hell did Lann and the others *do* to you?' He immediately regretted the question when he saw Ayla's reaction to the mention of her uncles.

Ayla's usually fiery-red hair was dulled with dirt. Her clothes, once a school uniform, were blackened and torn. Her skin was caked with muck, daubed here and there with blood from fresh grazes. All of her looked dark and ragged, all apart from her eyes which shone in almost unearthly contrast to the rest of her. She frowned. 'I don't know, Finny. I think they gave me something. Or they awakened something that was already there. Oh, I don't know. I can't explain it.'

I really can't, she thought. *It just seems … natural.*

In her usual practical way it was Benvy who broke the spell. 'Come on,' she said. 'We don't have time for this. We have to head on and see if we can find Sean.'

They passed the flame to two more torches and headed down the long passage.

Every few metres an arch was hewn into the wall, but whatever exit they had marked were lost now to piles of broken earth. Occasionally a new tremor knocked the group off their feet, and with every one they feared for Sean's safety. After following the passage for what seemed like hours, Ayla came to a stop. A few metres ahead, the passage turned sharply to the right. Directly in front of them, just before the turn, there was a crack in the wall.

'I know where we are,' Ayla said. There was no joy in her voice. 'We'd better hope we can go right. I do not want to go through that gap again. It was bad enough the first time.' The memory of icy water, of something grabbing her and dragging her under, made her almost sick. Waking up in the mouth of that toad had been nearly the most frightening experience of all. The goblins had rescued her, but only to deliver her to their master, the Red Root King. Her father. It still seemed impossible.

Turning the corner, they saw the roof of the tunnel had collapsed, and the way was blocked.

Then Benvy gasped. 'Look!' She pointed to the rubble. A black hand with long, gnarled fingers protruded from underneath the rubble. It was broken and limp.

'Poor girl,' Ayla said. 'She was just like us once. Now look at her.'

Finny and Benvy both struggled to imagine the gnarled, tar-skinned hand as ever having belonged to a normal girl, but they remembered how they had seen Ayla nearly turning into one of the goblins.

Now Ayla doubled back to the crack in the wall. The smell of cold dampness made her shudder. 'Get ready to swim,' she warned as she pushed herself through the fissure.

Sean didn't know it, but he was not far away from his friends. They were separated by metres of impassible rubble. He couldn't even be sure if they were alive or not. He was utterly, sickeningly afraid. Even when they had first entered the tunnels and he had become stuck, losing his grip on Benvy, he had at least known that his friends were up ahead and it was just a case of catching up with them. But now, he realised, they might all have been crushed by that last terrible aftershock. He could be truly alone in the dark.

Back when the chamber had fallen in on itself in a torrent of muck and rock, Sean had only just managed to escape with his own life, diving for the gap in the wall on his side. Once through the gap, he had had no choice but to fight his way through a tight space of rough, wet stone and thick, gnarled roots as a blast of scratchy dust from the imploding chamber rushed up from behind and engulfed him. The last frantic struggle to squeeze his way through had cut him painfully on the hip, but he had managed to reach another chamber. While he couldn't see much in the dim glow of the hammer, he could at least sense that the space was wide and high enough to stand for the first time since coming back down into this terrible, dangerous warren. He gave himself a moment and felt around his hip. The warm, damp patch on his shirt confirmed he had been bleeding, but while the cut stung badly he knew it wasn't a serious injury.

Sean tried hard to quell his sense of dread, but it was all consuming. He almost didn't want to lift the hammer up for fear of what he might see. His mind invented skulking phantoms with wide eyes and white-hot mouths. Tears rolled uninvited down his dirty cheeks, and he mumbled prayers that he might just wake up at home in his own room. But he was awake now, and a primal desire to survive drove him on to explore the dark chamber and find a way out, phantoms or not. He found a small gap where the wall – a bank of roots and muck – had been split under the weight of the collapsing roof. He tried not to think about what was probably a thousand tons of earth above his head. The gap had just enough give for him to pull it wider with effort but, before squeezing through, he poked the hammer through the gap to try and get a look at what lay in there.

Sean recognised the space as the small cell where they had found Ayla's phone. It was even smaller now, half-filled with rocks and broken roots. He yelped when he saw a goblin in the middle of the cell. Then he saw there was no light in its eyes. The goblin's neck was entangled in a root that had broken through the low ceiling, and it had choked, almost as if the vine had sought it out and strangled it. Black fingers still clung to the root where the creature had tried in vain to escape the root's murderous grip.

Sean held the hammer out and frantically searched for another exit. There was none – all of the other passages had been cut off. He felt a tremble in the ground and braced himself for another quake. Curling into a protective ball on the floor, he wiped tears from his cheeks and looked up instinctively to offer yet another prayer. Above his head he noticed an opening in the ceiling. He realised he might be able to reach it and leapt to his feet. The earth groaned and dirt fell from the ceiling with a whoosh. Sean stretched up as much as he could while trying to avoid the falling dirt getting in his eyes, but the opening stayed out of reach.

Another tremor nearly toppled him and some more of the cell's roof collapsed with roots snapping like bones. Sean had one more chance; he hunkered down and jumped, catching the lip of the hole with one free hand. How he managed it he didn't know, but with uncharacteristic grace and strength borne of sheer fear he swung the hammer up into the cavity and hauled himself up. He found it was only a tiny space, just high enough to crawl, but it seemed to go back a few metres, and there was nowhere else to go, so he started to shuffle and then scramble in panic as the ground fell away behind him. Sean used every bit of energy he had as the quake ate away mercilessly at his feet. It all happened so fast. His legs were sucked down but his hand clawed out to find purchase on a stone and again he found strength enough to heave himself up onto some kind of ledge. Everything behind him was swallowed into a void. Sean screamed against the cacophony until at last it waned and there was silence again. He waited and braced himself, telling himself he had to open his eyes again and move. He adjusted his glasses, smeared with dirt and sweat, which were half-hanging off one ear. The only way to go was to his left, through another tight gap. He squeezed himself though, wincing as his bloody hip was pressed into the rock and dirt. With his hammer behind him, it was completely dark and he moved forward very gingerly, but still found himself sliding down a sudden steep slope. Down and down he went, gathering pace to a dangerous headlong tumble. Every bend sent him careening against the side and fresh cuts opened all over him. At last, it levelled out and Sean's body rolled to a slow, unconscious stop.

CHAPTER 2

The Burning King

T ime is like a network of rivers flowing here and there at varying speeds. The friends had gone through days and nights of danger, but back in Kilnabracka it was still Saturday, only a few hours since the children had left with Ayla's uncles, Lann, Fergus and Taig, to the gates and into the alternate time of Fal. Sean's parents, Jim and Mary Sheridan, hung their wet coats on the old-fashioned coat stand in Greely's pub. Then Jim performed his traditional clap and rub of his hands before ordering their drinks.

'A white wine for the wife, Johno, and tell me this: is there any Guinness left?'

Jim always, without fail, asked if there was any Guinness left. The bar owner, John Greely just threw his eyes up and started pouring. Jim Sheridan was a creature of habit that was for sure and he never got tired of the same joke.

'Ah God, Jim, really? Every time?' Mary asked, exasperated.

'What?' her husband protested, and brought the drinks over to the table she had chosen, close to the fire. 'John, we'll both have the roast chicken with all the trimmings too, please.'

It was busy enough in the pub – the usual gaggle of men hunched over the bar, and women and couples at the tables enjoying the popular Kilnabracka tradition of a roast lunch in Greely's. Mary noticed that Old Podge Boylan was there – a permanent fixture – slurping his pints, in dire need of a bath and a shave. *Someone needs to look after that poor fella*, she thought.

Mary felt she would much rather be at home. But Jim was right: it was their first chance for a day out in ages, with Sean being away. It was just a shame that Greely's was his idea of a nice meal; a snazzy restaurant in Limerick would have been much better.

Podge was mumbling away to himself, which was par for the course. But he seemed a little more distressed than usual. He was a well-known character in Kilnabracka – once a famed herbalist and healer who used to work out of a big farm inherited from his father. He, and many Boylan men before him, had acres of plants and herbs there, all with secrets passed on from father to son for generations. But Podge lost the run of himself a bit and sold it years ago. Now he lived alone in a small cottage on the edge of Coleman's Woods and was rarely visited as the place tended to give people the creeps. It was laden with charms and dreamcatchers that tinkled and moaned hauntingly when the breeze passed through them. The subject of the old man's babbling was generally faeries and folklore and other such nonsense. On this occasion, however, his mumbling crescendoed to a rambling shout, and John Greely warned him that he was upsetting the other patrons.

'Bothering the udder patrons? Pah!' Podge shouted, turning around unsteadily on his stool. 'Ye are all in for it, I tell ya!' He finished with a few words in Irish that Mary couldn't quite catch – except for one: '*stoirm*' – storm.

He often meandered from English to Irish in mid-sentence, but never quite so menacingly.

'Ah quieten down, Podge, will you?' Jim said. 'I'm trying to have a nice drink with the wife.'

'Quieten down? Aaaaaach. *Amadán*! Something's goin' on with the magic folk! Have yiz not seen the mounds?'

'Podge, now, I'm warning you.' John Greely leaned over

the bar and put a hand on the old man's arm. 'You've had too much and you'll have to go home.'

Podge angrily shrugged off John Greely's hand and, in doing so, lost his balance and crashed to the floor. Some of the other patrons went to help him up.

'Gerroff me!' he shouted.

'Right, home!' John Greely had had enough. He was lifting the lid on the bar counter when the outside door swung open and a cold waft of air filled the place and cleared the turf smoke for a moment. It was the Mahoneys, parents of Brendan Mahoney, a boy in Sean's class.

'Ah, here!' Mr Mahoney exclaimed in a thick Dublin accent, undiluted by years of living in County Limerick. 'What's all this messin'?'

He spotted Jim and Mary Sheridan by the fire, and he and his wife edged around the chaos surrounding Podge to where the other couple were sitting.

'Aul Podge been at the sauce again, eh?' He winked at Jim, making a drinking motion and laughing just that bit too hard at his own wit.

'Sure, it happens to the best of us,' Jim replied. 'Could be us later on!'

Mary elbowed him in the side.

'It will not. We're out for a quiet one. I see you two are taking advantage of the school trip too?'

She had shuffled along to let Bridget Mahoney in beside her.

'Thanks, Mary,' said Bridget, taking off her coat 'Thank the Lord for the fire, it's freezing out there. What school trip?' she asked, raising her voice over the din at the bar, determined to ignore the kerfuffle with Podge. He was still writhing to get out from the grasp of two men.

'The Cashel trip. Is Brendan Jr not going? We decided a nice quiet drink and a bite to eat was in order, having the house to ourselves, especially on a Saturday afternoon.'

Bridget Mahoney grinned at the idea of the nice quiet drink, and her husband, Brendan Sr, interrupted, 'House to yourselves? Lucky you! We're payin' through the nose for a babysitter!'

'Mary, I never heard about any trip to Cashel.' Bridget was now registering what Mary Sheridan had said. 'Brendan Jr's at home. And he has a friend over from their class – the Dillon boy, Michael.'

Mary and Jim Sheridan looked at each other. Behind them, Podge was shouting something about 'the big fellas' now.

'The big fellas know all about them! They know what's going on. Yiz are all blind!'

'Hang on a sec, that can't be right!' said Jim, staring at the Mahoneys, confused.

Mary Sheridan's face darkened.

39

'I am going to kill him,' she said through gritted teeth. 'He's gone too far this time. Wait 'til I tell the Caddocks and Samantha Finnegan. I don't know what those little eejits are playing at, but they've lied to us!'

Then almost immediately her anger slid into worry. 'But where are they? Where have they gone off to? Oh, my God, Jim, Sean could be anywhere. We don't know where he is!'

In her fretting Mary hadn't noticed the scuffle with Podge had ended and the old man had calmed down. Now he was breathing heavily, staring at the four parents round the fire.

'Have those childer gone off with the big fellas?' he asked, wide-eyed.

'What does he mean, Jim? Is he talking about the Mac-Cormac brothers, Ayla's uncles?' Mary Sheridan's mind was racing with questions and confusion. 'Sure where would *they* be going? Why would our Seanie go off with them?'

'It's happening again! Circles within circles.' Podge sounded as though he was really rambling now.

'For God's sake, if I have to listen to this … *looper* … babbling any longer.' Mary Sheridan had tears in her eyes. 'Jim, get me home. We need to ring the Caddocks and Samantha Finnegan, see if we can find out what's going on.'

Podge had started to laugh, mostly to himself. Through a maniacal grin, he spouted out lines of some old poem:

'*When the Old Stones, faced with spiral line*
Glow along those ancient scores
The Daughter wrenched back to her time
By blackened claws through ancient doors
The heroes felled, their promise failed
As dead as autumn leaves
Then all is lost, the wind will wail,
To the storms that she will weave.'

Everyone in the pub fell silent as Podge spoke and, to Mary Sheridan, it even seemed as if the lights had dimmed and the fire lost some of its heat.

'Get me home, Jim,' she said, really starting to feel panic and pushing roughly past Podge Boylan to the door.

'Careful, Finny,' warned Ayla.

Back underground in the goblin tunnels, Finny was leading the little group down a tight shaft with his sword held out to see the way.

Ayla was trying to continue her warning. 'There's a steep bit and then a drop into water. Last time, I fell …'

But the warning was a moment too late. Finny slipped and hurtled down out of sight, his howl cut short with a large splash of water.

'Finny? Finny? Are you okay?' Ayla called down to her friend. She was worried, but there was an undeniable undercurrent of frustration there too. She couldn't help herself from thinking: *great, Finny, delay us some more, why don't you?*

'Argh! It's f… f… freezing!'

'Try to get to the edge,' Ayla shouted urgently. 'Find something to hold on to and wait for us there! It's not safe!'

Finny waded until he reached a damp embankment of stone. He held his sword out, disturbed by Ayla's cryptic words. *What did she mean, it's not safe?* His torch was floating, useless, on the water beside him.

After a minute, Ayla appeared through the gap Finny had just shot through; She let herself down with the help of Benvy and Benvy's javelin. Getting as low as she could, Ayla dropped into the water, managing to keep her torch above the surface, and emerged breathless with the cold.

Benvy followed, slipping down as carefully as she could, until finally she had to be coaxed into jumping. She shrieked at the impact of the icy pool; her flame, like Finny's, was snuffed out. Ayla and Finny pulled her over to the edge and helped her climb onto the ridge. They were all shuddering and shivering, but Ayla seemed to be especially shaky. She breathed deep, trying to control herself.

The water might be filled with them! Giant, hungry toads waiting to pull us under!

'We … We'll have to go under there.' She held her flame out towards the far end of the pool. The others could see that the cave roof sloped down to the surface and the water disappeared into the gloom underneath.

Ayla continued to explain how she knew where they needed to go next and why they had even more reason to be afraid, 'When I was here before, I was running from the goblins. I fell in here and … something grabbed me over there. I was pulled under. It …' She shook with bitter dread. 'I woke up and this thing was trying to *eat* me. An enormous, slimy toad! But the goblins killed it. That's when I was brought to the Red Root King, and that's pretty much all I remember after that.'

'When we were searching for you, we saw one of those toads!' Benvy said while trying to keep warm. 'It was dead: stripped to the bone. It was *gruesome*.'

'That must have been the one that the goblins killed.' Ayla was thinking out loud. 'So, we're close then.' *Closer to her. Closer to Maeve. Closer to killing her.* Ayla checked herself, disturbed again by the necessity to suppress her own thoughts. *Come on, Ayla, remember why you are down here. Save the goblins. Turn them back to girls. Find Sean. Get your best friends out of here alive! You can't lose them too. But I will sacrifice anything — anything — to get to Maeve and finish her.*

My mother. My evil, twisted mother.

'Yeah,' Benvy was still thinking back. 'That's where we found our way into that huge hall! The one where we found you on that big loom thing.' Then realisation dawned, and Benvy suddenly found herself very, very afraid of being in the water. 'But … Are there more of them in here?'

As soon as she asked the question, something fell with a plop into the pool beside them, sending ripples in arcs across the surface. All of them, even Ayla, let out a scream, and they huddled together shivering in the numbing wet. But they calmed when they saw more stones dropping into the pool; they'd been loosened from where Finny had fallen through.

Thinking about whether there were still more toads, Ayla had to admit, 'I don't know if there are any more. I honestly don't know. But there is no other way to get through. We have to dive under the rocks over there and swim through underwater. Once we're out the other side, we can get to that hall and the Red Root King's throne.'

Finny and Benvy were still unsure of exactly what Ayla was trying to do. 'And if we make it, and get to the throne, what then?' Finny asked. He had no real wish to go back there again. They had all been lucky to escape the last time. Just thinking about how they'd had to fight made his body ache where once there had been deep wounds. The goblins had been merciless when they caught him, and his battle with the Red Root King had taken a heavy toll on his body. He might not even have made it had it not been for Ayla's uncles.

'I'm not sure what will happen. I just know I have to find her,' Ayla answered.

'Find her?' Benvy queried. 'Don't you mean "them"? The goblin-girls? So we can save them? That's why we're down here, right?'

Once again, a burning temper flared in Ayla, from head to stomach. *No!* Her inner voice seethed. *You have no idea! There is no saving anyone! There is only finding Maeve.*

But outwardly Ayla just moved tentatively to the over-hang without saying anything. She looked back at her friends once, took in as much air as she could into her dust-sullied lungs and dived in to the deep, ice-cold water. Finny and Benvy looked at each other, swallowed hard and followed their friend into the night-black depths.

The last gulp of air was almost useless as instantly the freezing water nearly knocked all the breath out of them. Ayla hauled herself through with unnatural speed, fed by the determination that burned inside her. The fear of toads that might lurk in the black was just an unwelcome dis-traction. *They won't stop me.*

Benvy was the last to dive beneath the surface, and already her chest and throat were convulsing for breath as she struggled to keep up with Finny. The swim was difficult. With every aching effort to haul herself through the murky water, her panic increased. Her heart threw itself against her chest, and her neck clenched and unclenched, begging her to open her mouth and take in air. Just when Benvy was sure she could go no further, she made out Finny turning and coming back for her. He grabbed her by the collar and hauled her along. Benvy could feel her mouth wanting to open involuntarily. Then together the two kicked up and, at last, crashed through the surface in frenzied gasps for oxygen. Lying on the stone floor, heaving for air, Benvy hawked up a mixture of water and bile and then slumped, exhausted, by Finny's side.

When they felt ready to move again, Ayla tried in vain to repeat her trick of lighting the torch with her new-found powers. It was no use. Still numb with the cold, she couldn't focus, and each failed attempt only added to her increasing irritation. She was forced to give up, and Finny and Benvy used the dim light from their weapons to look around. They came upon the remains of the huge toad, slow to rot in the dank. It still stank enough to make them gag.

'That's where we went to get into the hall.' Benvy pointed to a small opening at the top of a slope. 'It was tight, and there's a hell of a drop to get in …' She stopped suddenly, remembering how she had fallen and how Sean had saved her. *I can't believe I left Sean behind. What was I thinking? Why aren't we looking for him? We should be looking for him.*

'Sean,' she said out loud to the others, and as she said his name she felt the threat of tears altering her voice. 'There's no sign of Sean.'

'I bet we'll find him in there.' Finny tried to reassure her. 'I bet he's in there, sitting on a rock, wiping his broken specs and wondering when we're going to bother showing up!'

But Benvy could see that Finny too was afraid for their friend.

'I really hope you're right, Finny,' Benvy murmured. At the same time, she turned, frustrated, and said, in an accusing way, mainly for Ayla's benefit, 'Anyway, last time, before me and Sean came in *here* we had already found what must have been the entrance to the hall. It was a huge steel door, out that way ...' She pointed to an opening halfway up the far wall, accessed by a sloping ledge. A fresh round of tremors shook the chamber and lethal chunks of stone dropped down in front of them. They all ran for the exit and clambered over the debris blocking the lower half of the opening just as the room caved in and the toad carcass was buried forever.

The friends emerged into a large vaulted space where the walls, covered in intricate and deeply peculiar mosaics, climbed high up to a ceiling that was impossible to see in the darkness. Benvy lead the way with the javelin, but there were also a few torches flickering on the walls for light.

Just ahead, the gargantuan remains of one of the Great Hall's steel doors loomed out of the black. It had fallen across the large chamber, wedging itself on the opposite wall. The carvings of goblin hordes that coursed along its surface were as disturbing as ever. The metal groaned occasionally, threatening to slip with the next tremor.

The other huge steel door hung precariously on twisted hinges. Through the great doorway nothing was visible. But there were sounds; the boom of crashing rocks echoed from the depths. The three friends looked at each other, silently resolving to enter the Great Hall and face whatever awaited them there.

The first thing they noticed were a number of fires. Far away, the other end was lit through a curtain of dust with orange flames. Many of the giant pillars in the hall, which once had soared up to the high ceiling, had collapsed, and mountains of broken earth were heaped high on either side of them. The air was filled with dirt, and the friends pulled their shirts over their noses to try and block out the worst of it. Here the tremors were more frequent, and every so often great boulders fell from the heights and pummelled the ground like stone bombs. Just then, one fell far too close with an explosion that knocked all three off their feet. They got up, regained their balance and looked to each other for an instruction, an idea, anything.

Ayla was rooted to the spot. Then her anger urged her forward: *Screw the danger! You will make it! Leave them!* But she fought it, wrestling with these terrible thoughts. *It's too dangerous! We'll all die!*

It was Finny who spoke first, and there was no doubting what he thought they needed to do next. 'Run!' he yelled, and he took off into the chaos.

He was fast, much more agile than the other two, but he stopped often to make sure they were still with him. As they sprinted through the Great Hall the ceiling continued to fall to the floor in giant chunks. Each time all three were thrown off balance; they had to scramble left and right to avoid falling pillars and mounds of earth that continued to crash down around them. They pulled each other through as best they could, and at last, and only just, they made it to the source of the fires.

The blaze was feasting on the remains of the Red Root King. The only part of him left intact was his head, now an effigy engulfed in fire. Behind it, his throne lay smashed, cleaved in three to form sheer cliffs of smooth granite. As suddenly as it had come, the violence of the earthquake subsided, and the friends could stop running and check each other for damage. There were some wounds, but none were too serious. Ayla's wound was the most painful-looking. A gash in her forehead was leaking blood in a bright trickle down her temple. But at least they were all in one piece.

They took in the scene around them, the king's burning head providing light from his last twisted grimace.

'What now?' asked Finny.

As his question hung in the air, a section of the king's burning remains fell to the ground in a burst of sparks, revealing the terrible wooden loom structure that Ayla had been strapped to. Though now the loom was different somehow – difficult to discern in the smoky firelight but certainly different.

'I can't go near that!' gasped Ayla, a sharp pain stabbing at her chest where once the contraption had attempted to extract her soul from her body. She turned away.

'Wait,' said Benvy, heading towards it. 'What's that on it?'

'Benvy, hold on!' Finny called after her. Reluctant to leave Ayla on her own, he said to her, 'Don't move. We'll be back in a sec'. I can see you from there. Just don't *move!*'

As Finny and Benvy drew closer to the remains of the awful contraption the full horror of the scene was exposed. Piled high on the wooden structure were bodies – dozens of them. The bodies were the remains of the poor goblin-girls, all lying prone, one on top of the other in a gro-tesque and frightening mound. The light in their eyes was gone. They were all dead.

'Oh, God!' Benvy exclaimed, grimacing but moving towards the horrifying sight.

'Benvy, don't go any closer!' Finny tried to stop her.

Shrugging Finny off and edging nearer to the mound of bodies, Benvy asked, horrified, 'What happened here?'

'*She* did this. Maeve did this,' said Ayla now beside them. She was looking up at the dreadful sight, all the while holding her chest as if it still hurt, even now.

'Those goblin-girls were all put on the loom and the last bit of life sucked out of them. For *her*. So she could gather just enough strength to escape. Whatever they had already taken from me allowed Maeve the strength to do that to them. She still may not be fully formed, but she is growing. And we *have* to get to her.'

Every fibre in my being tells me to get to Maeve. This is what my uncles died for. Nothing else matters.

Benvy couldn't help herself from continuing to gaze at the horrifying scene before her. She reached out a hand, extended a finger and touched one of the dead figures on the shoulder. The whole body simply fell apart beneath her touch as if it was made of sand. Benvy jumped back, frantically wiping her hand on her trousers.

'This is hell! We're in *hell*!' she screamed. 'The swim, the earthquakes, the toad's carcass, the fire and now this!' It was all too much. Most of all, the loss of Sean was draining her of any will to go on. Benvy was losing her grip, slipping into complete despair. Everything that had happened since that day in Coleman's Woods was just too much. The nightmare was engulfing her.

I can't take this anymore! I want to go home! Her mind screamed. *Why can't we just get Sean and go home!*

'Benvy, it's okay. We'll be alright!' Finny tried to calm her. He could see his friend was really struggling, sobbing without tears. Her eyes were wide and darting around, and she held her sandy waves in tight clumps, as if she might tear them from her scalp.

'Benvy! Please!' Finny continued to try to get through to Benvy.

Ayla said nothing. She was horrified that she was the cause of all this pain, but she was angry too, angry at Benvy's weakness, and impatient, always impatient to get moving.

Just then, a familiar voice interrupted them all, directing itself at Benvy. 'Well, you were the last one I thought would fall apart. I thought that would be me. I was odds-on favourite, defo.'

All three friends turned to face the direction of the croaky voice and saw Sean's familiar figure emerging from the shadows. He walked directly to Benvy and put his arms around her.

'Now, get a grip on yourself, Caddock,' he said, smiling

at his friend. 'We'll get out of this yet.'

At first Benvy just stared at him, completely stunned – they all were. Then she grabbed him to make sure he was real, hugged him until he was beginning to feel half-strangled, and finally she clattered him across the back of the head.

'Sheridan, you *plonker*!' Benvy cried and then laughed, hugging him again. 'I could kill you!'

Finny ran over too and clipped his friend over the ear playfully. After a moment, Ayla seemed to snap out of her daydream and she joined in the group embrace.

'How did you? Where have you been? What the hell *happened*?' they shouted all at once.

'Follow me,' Sean said in reply. 'I think you'll want to see this.'

CHAPTER 3

The Toad Pit

Ayla, Benvy, Sean and Finny reached the foot of the throne. Above them, the rockface rose up into the vast cavern, its sides scarred and cleaved by the shaking of the earth tremors. The group made their way hastily down past the soaring, disintegrating walls to a place where the ground descended steeply.

'We'd better not hang around!' Finny warned. They felt the ground tremble in warning of another quake and ran.

Behind them, the once-great hall began its final crumble

and, in a deafening bellow of crushing rock and surging earth, the huge cavern collapsed in on itself. The destruction blew a surge of flying debris after the friends, who were saved from being struck by the way the path sloped downwards. They clambered down over the smooth rock, having to half-slide on their backsides where there was no grip and it was too steep. At last they reached a point where the steep slope levelled out, and before them was another cave mouth.

'Sean, where are we going?' Finny asked.

'Just wait 'til you see this' was all their friend would say.

They walked through the cave, and collectively gasped. Gone were the walls of root and mud. Gone were the tight dusty tunnels and rough-hewn, rocky, narrow passages. Before them lay a vast chamber, quite different from all that they had encountered so far. Here the ceiling was domed, its curved surface decorated with the most intricate carvings of goblins and what seemed to be children. The children were all girls. Each girl was flanked by two grown-ups, but the depiction of the adults was all wrong – they were ridiculously tall and, even stranger, all sported antler-like horns.

The whole of the dome was lit by a shimmering blue aurora. The walls of the chamber were just as astounding. Dozens of arches were hewn out of the sides; each one led either to an ornate doorway or window. The

arches themselves were framed either side by columns of immense bones; the doors and windows were all set beneath what looked like carved images of angry eyes and snarling lips so the openings resembled mouths. The whole effect was one of hundreds of enormous, gaping faces staring out at anyone within the chamber.

Sean urged the group forward. 'Careful now! There's quite a drop coming up ahead.'

The three walked across the flat stone, resisting the temptation to keep staring up and back at the dark maws of the faces, and instead watched their footing. They reached an edge where the stone floor simply stopped and they could see what Sean meant.

Finny was the last to look over. 'Oh, jaypers, I'm going to be sick.'

The others gave him a surprised look. Finny rarely admitted weakness. He was the real sporty one among them, fit as a fiddle. Finny was never afraid of anything.

'What? I don't like heights, alright?'

'This would make anyone feel woozy!' Sean grinned as he watched the others' similar reaction.

The sides of the huge circular cavern appeared to fall away for hundreds of metres, the pattern of bone pillars and grotesque windows repeating themselves uninterrupted until they finally reached a broad, round lake of shimmering blue at the bottom – the source of the aurora that shone on the domed ceiling above, and danced in reflections on all other surfaces within the chamber. The water was aglow with some sort of ghostly phosphorescence.

'How did you find this place?' Finny asked Sean, who was looking quite proud of himself. 'Wait. Start from the beginning. What the hell *happened* to you?'

At this, Sean's face darkened. 'It wasn't fun. How I made it, I'm not sure. I nearly didn't a couple of times.'

Sean went on to recount how he had found Ayla's old cell, with the body of a goblin inside, and how he barely escaped there with his life.

'I slid down some passage in the dark for ages. Then I must have been knocked out, because I woke up in total blackness and didn't have a clue where I was. For a minute I couldn't remember what had happened at all! That was pretty damn scary, let me tell you. Waking up in a place like this and not knowing why you're there is so not nice.'

'Well, I know how that feels,' Ayla interjected.

Remembering then Ayla's terrible underground ordeal, Sean was a little embarrassed.

'Of course you do, sorry Ayls,' Sean said, sheepishly. Ayla's smile let him know it was okay to continue.

'So then, after a while, it all came flooding back. I sat for a bit and tried to get my head together. I was pretty banged up too. I had gotten this earlier and the fall only made it worse.'

He showed them the gash on his hip. It was caked in dry blood, and his shirt and jeans were matted with dried blood too. They winced in sympathy.

'I had the hammer for light, and there was only one direction I could go in, so I took it. It led down, pretty steeply at times, but thankfully I didn't slip again. A couple of times the tremors hit and I was nearly buried, but some kind of blind luck kept the whole place from collapsing on me. I even managed to hold on to these.' He pointed to his glasses, with the one remaining lens still only slightly scratched.

'The passage was super-tight at times and I really had to squeeze through. Then, it got a little wider. But the wide bits were just as scary, with those horrible, bloody carvings.' At this, he shuddered.

Benvy piped up. 'Sheridan, you must have nearly wet yourself. From being scared of a forest path to this? Holy moly!'

'Yeah,' Sean grinned. 'I'll tell you what – I'll never be scared of the woods again after this. If we ever get back there …

'Anyway, I eventually came to a couple of big rooms. They were more … ornate than the rest of the place. Like, there were pillars and arches, a bit like those …' He pointed to the sides of chamber they were in, '… but smaller. The rooms stank to high heaven. It was rancid. One had these vats, sort of like big barrels, filled up with this horrendous *gunge*. It smelled like rotten eggs.'

Ayla interrupted again. 'That was their food! That was what they fed me. And what eventually got me out of there. Something about the smell made me think of flammable stuff. I took a chance, waited for them to come in to the cell for one of their regular taunting sessions, and grabbed one of their torches. I got this for my trouble.'

She showed them the burn on her arm where one of the goblins had bitten her. They could see the faint scar that was left after her uncles' healing.

'Thankfully the stuff was more than flammable. It was like a bloody flash grenade! It blinded the lot of them and I got out.'

'Wow! Fair play to you, Ayls. But, ugh! *Gross*! I thought it was their toilet. I don't know how you ate that stuff!'

At the mention of eating, they all remembered how hungry they were by now but they tried to ignore it.

Sean continued: 'Well, I followed the path through these two rooms. The second one was definitely a kitchen. It had a pit with the embers of a fire and slabs of some kind of meat hanging over it.'

'The toad!' Benvy guessed.

'Oh, really? Toad?' Sean didn't seem happy about this

information. 'I wish you hadn't mentioned that.'

'Why?' Finny asked.

Sean opened his shirt and pulled out two large hunks of the burnt meat. He took two more pieces from his pockets.

'Because I figured we were going to need to eat something, and I was hungry so I took some. I didn't really think about what it might be. *Bon appétit?*' He offered each of them one of the hunks of burnt meat.

The friends looked at each other, curling their lips. But their stomachs protested and, without thinking, they took the meat and tore it apart, dividing it between them. They ate hungrily at first, then gagged.

'How can it still be so ... *slippery*, even after it's cooked?' asked Benvy, shuddering.

'It's vile,' Finny said. 'But thanks.'

'Aren't you having some?' Ayla asked Sean, spitting flecks of toad at her feet.

'Nah, I ate about half a kilo of the stuff in the kitchen.'

Sean continued with his story. 'So I followed a corridor that lead directly to the throne. I saw the loom, the burning roots. I saw that the hall was falling apart. At that point I nearly did too. I didn't think we were going to make it. I thought I was going to die down here, alone. So I did a little exploring, just to get away from there, and I found this place. Then I heard you, Benv'. And, well, here we are.'

'So what now?' Benvy asked.

'Now we go down again,' Ayla said.

'How about a bit of a rest?' Finny asked. He was exhausted.

'I can think of nicer places to sleep,' said Sean. 'But at this stage I'd sleep in one of those barrels of poo.'

'Gross, Sheridan. But he's right Ayla,' Benvy added. 'We need to have a rest, get some strength back. I might even try to swallow a bit more of that minging toad-meat.'

Ayla relented. 'A short rest then.'

They found a corner where at least their backs weren't exposed. They ate a little more, deciding unanimously to save some for the journey ahead. Finny announced he would take first watch, as even in the deathly quiet they didn't feel safe. But it didn't take long for Finny to give in to the struggle, and soon he too was deep in exhausted sleep.

In the good room at the Sheridans' house, the clock on the mantelpiece ticked noisily. The children's families had come together to speak with local Garda Pat Kelly about their disappearance.

Both Benvy's parents, the Caddocks, and Finny's mum, Samantha, had refused the offer of tea, but the Guard was happy enough to let Jim Sheridan refill his cup. He was partly buying for time – a ploy he often used to glean more information during interviews. *Say nothing. Let them talk. Works every time.* He took another biscuit too.

Mary Sheridan broke the long silence. 'Is the tea okay, Pat?'

'Lovely tea, thank you,' he confirmed.

'Our pleasure,' Mary replied. 'Now, how will you go about finding our children?'

The policeman seemed displeased at the directness of her tone. He preferred to be in charge of questioning.

'You'll recall, Mrs Sheridan, that this is not my first time visiting your home in relation to your son? And that last time I drove out here it was a wasted journey.'

'Yes, I recall. I'm sure it looks bad, but now they really are missing.'

'Please, Pat,' Una Caddock interjected, 'As you can imagine, we're very worried.'

'I can imagine,' he replied, 'but I assure you, this sort of thing with children of this age is not out of the ordinary. They will most likely be home tonight, feeling a little worse for wear, and ye can tear into them then. Now, young man.'

He nodded to Mick Caddock, Benvy's brother, who was reaching for another biscuit. His mother brushed the boy's hand away.

'Michael! Would you get your priorities right and answer the man! Half of this is your fault.' She regretted saying this almost instantly; worried that it might implicate her son. 'Well, I mean of course you had nothing to … Look, just answer the Guard!'

'Oh, eh … sorry. What?'

The Guard stared at Mick for a while. 'You say you were an accomplice in their desertion? That you drove them to the Rathlevean estate, to where one …' He checked his notes, '… Ayla MacCormac resides, being a friend of the missing children.'

'Well, I m … mean,' Mick stuttered, afraid now that he was in proper trouble. 'I don't know about "accomplice"! I gave them a lift, that's all!'

'But you knew there was no school trip? And, in fact, you pretended to be the children's teacher in order to deceive your parents and Sean Sheridan's parents.'

Mick blushed. 'Yes.'

Mrs Caddock just managed to stop herself giving her son a clip. *How could he be so stupid?*

His father lost the plot. 'You little …' he shouted, 'you'd better bloody well tell us everything you know or so help me I'll give that car to charity!'

'Thank you, Mr Caddock,' the guard intervened. 'If Michael could just answer my questions. Now, Ayla Mac-Cormac lives at No. 13, Rathlevean, with her uncles …'

He checked his notes again. 'Lann MacCormac and his brothers Fergus and Taig. Local builders.'

'Yes.' Mick was wishing he was anywhere else but here. *What did I let Benvy persuade me to do that for?*

'And was there anyone there, in the house, when you dropped them off?'

'I dunno. I just dropped them off at the top of the road. Then I came home. Look, I'm sorry I did the teacher thing! But I thought they probably just wanted to have a party or something!' Mick couldn't help thinking the adults were all overreacting. 'We were all young once, right?' He searched all their faces for affirmation, but was met only with scowls.

'You're still young, you little pup!' Una Caddock was getting even angrier as she realised Mick wasn't taking them that seriously and her own fears were growing by the minute.

Garda Kelly took his time in answering. 'In my experience, lad, you are probably right. However, given that your parents have tried to contact the MacCormacs to no avail and the men's whereabouts are indeed currently unknown, this will require some further enquiries on my part. In the meantime, I suggest you leave the official investigation to us and stay home by the phone in case they call. Lost children invariably do.'

He stood up from the chair, and pulled on his hat.

'Thank you for the tea, Mrs Sheridan. I'll be in touch. I'm sure this whole business will sort itself by morning.'

He took another biscuit before Mary Sheridan escorted him to the door. When she had closed it behind him, Jim thought his wife looked frail.

'They'll call, love.'

'Yes. Please God.' Then Sean's mother paused for a moment. 'Jim, can you stay here? I'm going to see Podge Boylan. I think he knows something about the MacCormacs. Maybe if we can find them, we can find out where the children have gone.'

In the cold blue light of the vast goblin chamber Ayla heard it first. Then they all did, sitting up with a jolt. A long, loud screech, echoing up from the depths.

'Holy …!' Sean exclaimed. 'What the flip was *that*?'

'I'm not sure but it sounds like one of the goblins,' Ayla replied. 'Get your stuff together.'

'Oh, God, Ayla, can't we just get out of here? Can't you magic us out, or something?' Benvy asked. The reason why they were down here again had never stopped tapping at her like a stubborn moth against a window pane. 'We got Sheridan back, now let's not push our luck anymore. Can't we just go home?'

Ayla wanted so much to go home. To be back in Kilnabracka, sitting in the back of her uncles' rickety old jeep, bouncing home to a hot stew and TV with Fergus and Taig. But all of that was over. Home was gone. The only thing that existed was here. The more she accepted this, the more energised she felt.

'I told you,' Ayla replied. 'We can't stop. That noise might be something to do with *her*. If I could send you back I would, Benvy, but I just can't. I have to find Maeve. I just do. I can't explain it. You just have to trust me, and you have to come with me. So please, *please*: stop whining and *COME ON!*'

She shouted the last two words, her temper at last breaking the surface. The others were shocked. It was totally unlike Ayla to get so angry. Benvy, for once, was lost for words.

Ayla had sprung to her feet and was already walking towards the yawning chamber. Resigned to following his friend, Finny sighed, and picked up his sword. He urged Benvy and Sean to come along with a nod of his head as he jogged after Ayla's retreating form.

'Ayla, wait!' he called out to her as quietly as he could. 'Can we think about this? And can we calm it down? I'd rather not invite whatever it is up here to meet us.'

She ignored him. 'Look: over there.' Ayla pointed to the left, to a flat shelf descending along the wall in a series of huge, wide steps. 'Come on!' she urged, running to the edge. The others had no choice but to follow, struggling to keep up.

At each stair there was a drop of almost two metres. Ayla didn't wait for help in getting down; she hung by her fingers and dropped, not hesitating even for a second before rushing to the next stair. It was more difficult for the others, given the awkward weapons they had to carry. They called after her but were ignored.

They could see now that the staircase spiralled down among the elaborate colonnades, flattening out every so often to form broad balconies, flanked by numerous windows and doors, before breaking into steps again until it reached the lake at the bottom. It became noticeably colder the further down they went, and by the time they reached the first balcony, even the effort of climbing down and running along couldn't keep them from shivering. Now close-up, the full scale of the façade could be appreciated. It was obvious these structures were not designed to house just the goblins. This was a palace for the Red Root King, and the cruel-looking edifices were simply dizzyingly huge. It made the whole experience all the more petrifying.

About halfway to the bottom, the group heard the piercing shriek again. It reverberated off the cold, bone-shaped pillars so that it seemed like a multitude of invisible creatures were hollering at the gang from the shadows. Finny, Benvy and Sean descended another flight of giant steps, and finally caught up with Ayla. Her eyes were blitzing with sparks again. She had only paused for a heartbeat, to make sure her friends were keeping up, before disappearing through a gaping doorway in one of the colossal archways into the gloom beyond.

'Ayla, for God's sake, wait!' Finny shouted after her.

They followed her through the arch into a huge corridor. It was even colder in here, and the air moved through it in a moaning, ghostly draft. There was no telling how high up the ceiling was. They felt like ants in a cathedral. This time Ayla did stop, and turned sharply to face her friends. Hissing with pure anger, she declared, '*She*'s here!' With the unnatural light seering out from her eyes, Ayla made a deeply unsettling sight.

This is not Ayla, Finny thought.

With that, Ayla took off again and her friends had to sprint to keep up with her, following the fizzing trail of sparks that cascaded from her eyes as she ran. They all held their weapons out, not just to see but to be ready for whatever fight faced them. Ayla lit the gloom around her like a fireball and they caught glimpses of gargantuan statues lining the walls – cloaked and hooded figures staring at them with dead eyes. All the statues were variations of the same person: a woman with a harsh angular face set eternally into a kind of sneer. Ayla recognised her instantly. They were all effigies of Maeve.

The group reached another doorway that led down to a new set of steps. They lowered themselves as quickly as they could and found themselves on yet another balcony. This one looked out on a totally new chamber, wide and cylindrical too, but lit this time with thousands of torches. The ceiling disappeared way above them. The screeching they could still hear was coming from far below.

Tentatively, they approached the edge where Ayla was standing between two of the tall bone-columns that seemed to be a recurring feature of this underground palace. Sean noticed out of the corner of his eye another great stone chair, similar to the one from the Red Root King's Great Hall, set into the wall beside the steps, and he pointed it out to Benvy.

'What is this place?' she asked, but no one had an answer to that.

The walls here were lined with more balconies, holes and tunnels, but these were rough-hewn and human-sized. This time, the bottom was not far below, only thirty metres or so. The floor was circular, surrounded with torches that burned either side of several dark arches. The bottom was concave, like a sort of pit, and covered in sand, much of which was darkened with splashes of what the friends assumed had to be blood.

In the middle of this pit, one of the goblins was standing, frantically screeching and turning in every direction to face four fat, oozing, rhino-sized toads, which were slowly circling their prey on the slopes, all the while edging closer.

CHAPTER 4

The Wrong Reflection

'What should we do? Should we help her?' Finny was asking Ayla, who was now looking downcast and almost disinterested in the fate of the goblin below. She didn't even bother to answer Finny.

The voice in her head was dismissive, almost bored. *It's not her. This is a waste of time.*

'Ayla! What should we *do*?' Finny asked again. Benvy and Sean threw him troubled glances. Ayla was behaving very strangely.

'I thought it was *her*,' Ayla said, closing her eyes. They had returned to normal, the strange spark extinguished.

'Yes, well, it's *not*,' Benvy said. 'It's one of those goblin things we're supposed to have come down here to save. Right? The only one alive we've come across. So ... do you still want to save her?'

Ayla didn't say anything. She stared at the scene below and didn't even flinch as the cornered creature let out another piercing howl.

Benvy looked to the others for support. They shrugged, unsure of what to do. She threw her eyes up and groaned, 'Look, Ayla, you said they're girls that were trapped like you were, and we have to save them. So we came down here and nearly died so we can do that. But if you're not going to help ....' She held her javelin up in her right hand. 'Then *feck* it, *I'll* do it!'

Benvy turned, drew back the javelin and threw it as hard as she could in the direction of the nearest toad. The sound was deafening, the light blinding. The weapon flew as screaming, red lightning that made them all cover their eyes and ears in pain. It hit the nearest toad in the back, and the monster exploded in sloppy chunks, leaving behind a smoldering black hole. The javelin was halfway into the ground. The other three toads opened their mouths and made a guttural, glugging, throaty *honk*, but still plodded relentlessly towards the now-prone goblin. Unconscious, it lay at the bottom of the pit, its gnarled hands still cover-ing its face.

'Oh, God, I've probably killed *it* too,' Benvy said, when the ringing in her ears had stopped and the sunspots had stopped dancing.

Finny and Sean looked at Benvy in shock, and then at each other. In response, Sean hoisted his hammer. 'Right, well,' he said, almost matter-of-factly. 'Best get down there then.'

For a moment, the others hesitated. They weren't used to this new, decisive version of Sean. It was usually Finny who was the man of action; his motto was definitely 'when in doubt, act'.

With Finny and Benvy following behind, Sean ran past the huge chair on his right and, as he went, he noticed a small recess in the stone at its feet.

'This way!' he shouted.

The small recess led to a short passage and a normal-sized staircase that descended to a tunnel below. To the left, this tunnel opened into the sandy arena in front of the goblin. Sean came to a sudden stop just at the bottom of the stairs, his friends crashing into his back. They man-aged to haul him back before he toppled out into the open. Looking back down the tunnel they were now in, they could see a line of toads marching slowly towards the opening to the pit. All in all, they counted seven.

'Er,' Sean said, beginning to slightly regret his sudden moves. 'Well, that's now ten toads altogether. *Ten!* How're we going to … Ah, *screw it!*' He made his decision and swivelled to face one of the approaching toads, raising his hammer over his head. Catching sight of Sean and the others, the ugly creature licked its lips with a long, black tongue and then opened its mouth to strike just as Sean brought his weapon, now ablaze with light, down on its head. Like Benvy's javelin, the weapon had magical properties other than being a pretty useless torch; it could cause devastating damage to anything it struck. The beast was crushed to pulp in an instant, and the iron fist of the hammerhead continued through to the ground beneath it in one swoop. A shockwave pulsed out, and Sean was lifted off his feet; four more toads behind it were hurled against the rippling walls of the tunnel and their bodies crushed against it. Finny and Benvy were flung back painfully against the steps.

Finny was the first to struggle to his feet, massaging his limbs back into action. He checked that Benvy was okay and, finding her confused but unhurt, he limped down the tunnel to where Sean was now grappling with the half-buried hammer. The entire passage was coated with the gruesome remains of toad. That left two who had made it to the opening to the pit, with three left in the pit itself. Five more to face.

'I'd love to find a way to use this thing that *doesn't* result in a giant explosion followed by a need to dig it out of the ground,' Sean said.

Finny didn't have time to help. He was running towards the two toads at the tunnel entrance, pointing his sword ahead, ready to thrust into their flesh. He was thinking about hurling: scooping up the ball with his hurl and flicking it up in the air. He had mastered this, so that he could run at full pelt and flick the ball up every time. He drove the blade forward and it sang as it sliced the air, glowing blue and lengthening so that it pierced both toads from back to front. In one motion, Finny pulled it up and the sword cleaved through the monsters' backs with no resistance. Jumping over the carcasses, Finny carried on into the pit.

'Three left!' he shouted over his shoulder.

Benvy had managed to help Sean haul the hammer from the dirt and the two ran to join Finny. There were indeed three more toads, the largest of which was now right beside the goblin's limp body, running a fat tongue along it. The toads were sluggish creatures, and Benvy skipped easily past the closest to reach her javelin. From across the pit another toad shot out its long tongue, and Benvy realised it was stuck between her shoulders, dragging her backwards. She just succeeded in freeing her red-gold spear from the sand before the toad began dragging

her towards its wide, gaping mouth. Benvy twisted herself round and pushed her weapon deep into the flesh
between the toad's giant beady eyes.

Sean appeared by her side and helped her to her feet.
Meanwhile, Finny was running towards the centre.

'One more down, two to go!' yelled Sean.

No sooner had he said this than another toad-tongue
caught Finny on the ankle just as he was closing on the
goblin and the huge, fat toad in the centre of the pit. Finny
felt himself being hoisted into the air. He was held aloft
for a second, just long enough for him to stab his sword
downwards, the blade extending as it went. There was a
sickening sluicing sound as the sword shot cleanly through
the head of the mutant toad that had been readying itself
to eat the goblin. But Finny was still held in the air by a
long, warty tongue.

For the moment, the goblin was safe. The only toad left
was the brute that had hold of Finny and was now dangling the boy over its yawning jaws. Finny was only inches
from the slimy orifice when a hot bolt of lightning struck
the side of the toad and the beast simply exploded.

Ayla was standing on the edge of the balcony high above
the scene with her hands stretched out, her eyes burning
with white fire and a rumbling, angry storm cloud writhing above her head. The dead toad's severed tongue was
still burning the skin on Finny's ankle and thrashing about

as though alive until, finally, Finny managed to cut through it with his sword and it fell from his leg, completely lifeless.

All of the toads were dead. When Finny, Benvy and Sean had dusted themselves off and checked that they weren't seriously wounded, Ayla joined them in the pit.

'I'm sorry, guys,' she said, more to herself. 'I should have been down here with you. I just …' She found she couldn't finish. She didn't know what to say, how to explain. *What is wrong with me?*

'It's okay. You saved me, so thanks,' Finny reassured her.

'What are we going to do with *that*?' Sean asked, pointing towards the unconscious goblin.

Ayla approached the creature, and knelt at its side.

'Careful, Ayla!' Finny urged.

'It's okay. I need you all to come here.' She gestured. 'Kneel beside her, in a circle. That's it.'

The creature began to wake.

'Quickly! Grab an arm, a leg! You'll need all of your strength!'

The goblin's eyes opened into those ghostly moonlike orbs. Its mouth gaped, shimmering the air with heat. With a low growl, the creature jerked to life, threshing like a landed shark. It took an enormous effort to hold it down while Ayla began to hum. Her voice was inhumanly deep.

I don't know how I'm doing this, she thought. *I just know I can.*

With one hand free, she began to pull a string of light from her chest, placing it on the goblin. Then she reached out and pulled a similar light from each of her friends. Sean and Benvy flinched, unsure if they should allow this to happen. It was just as Lann, Fergus and Taig had done back when they had saved Ayla, what seemed like an age ago, and the big fellas had died doing it. Finny urged them to trust in Ayla. Her three friends cried out in pain while Ayla's chant grew ever louder. The torches that lined the walls wavered and then dimmed. The little group seemed surrounded by a veil of shadow, lit only by the threads, spooling from their bodies.

The goblin still struggled with all its strength, but the blackness of its skin was beginning to recede. The change started at its fingers and toes, revealing slender, pale hands and feet. Then the black retreated across its body and up its neck, at last unveiling a human face. It was indeed a young girl.

Finally, before they were drained completely, Ayla waved a hand through the blinding strings of light to release them from the girl. They all promptly fell back onto the bloody dirt, senseless but still alive.

The group had no way of knowing how long they had been unconscious. Finny was the first to stir, waking with a start, and immediately fearful of more toads or goblins. There was a point on his chest which ached as if he had been punched, and the skin on his ankle had swelled up in an angry blister from the toad's tongue but, for the most part, he was all right, and they were alone in the pit for the time being at least. The others woke too and sat up groaning and clutching their chests. Ayla was the last to stir, and it looked like the whole ordeal had taken the most out of her. She bent over and threw up.

'Are you going to be okay?' Finny asked her, putting a hand on her shoulder.

'I'll be fine. But, where is she? The girl?'

Finny had totally forgotten about the goblin-girl. The friends all struggled to their feet and looked around, but there was no sign of her among the sloppy remains of the giant toads.

'She could be anywhere!' said Sean. 'Anyone know how long we were out?'

'I don't think it was long,' answered Benvy. 'There's still smoke coming from that toad that Ayla hit.'

Finny, Benvy and Sean looked at Ayla with a mix of admiration and nervousness. She was becoming less and less the friend they knew, and more and more something or someone else.

'That was … pretty impressive,' Finny said. 'But maybe you could give us some warning next time you decide to blow something up with lightning from your eyeballs.'

'I've seen more stuff like that. When I was in Fal the last

time. The guy who helped me and Fergus with the Normans – remember I told you about him – Goll. He could
do that stuff. Pulling storms from the sky. Man, I would
love to be able to do it!' said Sean. 'But, how? What's going
on with you, Ayls?'

'I'm not sure, Sean,' Ayla answered honestly. 'It only
seems to happen when I really need it, and then I just
know what to do.' *It flows through me*, she thought. *Flows
through me like hot lava. It hurts so much. But a good hurt. It
feels … like power.*

Of course it does, her other voice said. *Your power is growing.*
This time it really felt like someone else was talking to her.
Someone else was invading her thoughts, wresting control
from her. *Who are you? Why is this happening to me?*

Because, it answered, *you are my daughter.*

Before Ayla had a chance to respond, Benvy suddenly pointed. 'Look, up there in the tunnel!'

Cowering under one of the arches to the left of them
was the girl. Now they could see her more clearly, they
could see she was short and willowy, with tangled, matted
black hair. She was also filthy, but wherever there was a
gap in the film of dirt, her skin was chalk-white. The little
figure was cowering down, holding her face in her hands,
too petrified to look around.

Benvy made her way up the slope of the pit and approached
her, slowly. 'It's okay. We won't hurt you,' she urged.

The others hung back, watching as Benvy held out her hand. The girl slunk further back into the passage beyond the archway.

'Wait! It's really okay. I promise. We're here to help you.'

The girl's dark eyes stared down at the rest of them, and they did their best to smile reassuringly. Sean waved, not realising how frightening he looked, all covered in gore and holding a hammer almost as big as himself.

Suddenly making up her mind, the girl sprang up and disappeared down the dark passage.

'Wait!' Benvy shouted after her. 'Guys, come on!'

'No!' shouted Ayla.

Benvy looked incredulous. 'What? Ayla, we're going to lose her!'

'We have to find her, Ayla,' Sean agreed, and he started up the slope towards the passageway.

'No! Look … We … Finding Maeve is all that matters now.' *How can I explain this? I can't even explain it to myself. She just spoke to me! I feel like I'm a passenger in my own mind.*

'We've failed those girls already. Maeve took them and sucked the last bit of life out of them. You saw the results! They're just husks! By now she is probably just strong enough to escape. I can finish her – I *know* I can! That is what I'm *meant* for. I'm the only one who can stop her! If we find the girl on the way, then great. But nothing more can get in the way of what I have to do. *Please*. I need your help.'

Ayla wasn't sure of her own words. She wasn't sure she was even saying them.

'So everything else gets sacrificed for your new *mission*?' Benvy argued. 'Sean was expendable. We could just leave him behind in the dark? "Nothing can stop us," you said! And now this little girl, who is scared half to death, alone in this *horror*, and we're supposed to just leave her too?'

Finny piped up. 'Benvy, I don't like this either. But there is a bigger picture here which maybe we just can't understand. You've seen what Ayla can do now. She has some kind of power, and she has to have it for a reason. We should do what she says – otherwise we may never get home! Also, how do we know that girl is good? How do we know she's not just a goblin in a girl's body?'

'Oh right, Finnegan! She really looked dangerous, shivering with fright, not knowing where the hell she is!' Benvy retorted.

'Look, it's obvious Ayla has some higher purpose,' Sean said, 'But we came down here to save some kids. And now we're letting the only one we managed to save go! We may never make it home now, and for what?'

'I will get us home,' Ayla promised. 'But there won't be one to go to if I don't finish this.'

Mary Sheridan had driven a couple of miles out of town to the far side of Coleman's Woods. She hoped against hope that Podge Boylan had been driven home and was sleeping off the effects of his outburst in Greely's. She had to leave her car parked on the verge and walk the rest of the way to Podge's cottage. The small cottage could only be accessed by an overgrown lane; once fit for carts and horses but long since engulfed by nature. A gate, brown with rust, hung crookedly between moss-laden stone walls and the path disappeared behind it into the spinach-green forest. It was not a comforting place, but Sean's mother swept aside any apprehension, determined to find out what the old lunatic knew about Ayla's uncles and their connection to her missing son.

It was late afternoon on a wet, leaden October Saturday. The light was too weak to penetrate the canopy and, at times, the path was dark as night, but she could hear strange noises. From the branches odd-looking charms knocked together in tuneless, shrill dings, like a warning. Sean's mother ignored the urge to turn away and pushed on through the tall, wet grass until the trees parted and she was in the grey daylight again. The cottage hunkered in an unkempt field, surrounded by the woods. Its thatch was fresh enough but the whitewash was peeling from walls distorted by age. The small windows were black, shrouded by eves, and both halves of the warped door were shut.

Around the building, stones of various size jutted from the grass, blotched with white and black markings, and all scored with decorative lines. One or two sported distorted faces, locked in permanent grimaces that made Sean's mother's heart thud even harder. She knocked on the door and called out, but there was no answer. To add to her sense of foreboding, it had started to rain.

She tried the door; it wasn't locked, and after a couple more knocks she decided to open it and have a look inside, just to be sure Podge wasn't around. A wall of pungent smells hit her as soon as she entered the cottage; the air was heavy like musty soup. She had to brush aside huge bushels of dried leaves that hung on string from the rafters of the low ceiling. The house was the very definition of sparse, with no comforts save a wooden chair by a cavernous hearth, where the turf billowed smoke anywhere but up the chimney. In the centre of the room was a table with a large pestle and mortar and an array of empty bottles, all bearing the labels of various distilleries. More bottles were scattered about the stone floor. Aside from that, there was a basin and a jug, and a rickety ladder going up to a platform where, she presumed, Podge slept off the effects of the whiskey.

Through a dirty window on the other side of the cottage, Sean's mother spotted the old man. His hunched back was just visible over the tips of the grass where he squatted in front of one of the largest stones scattered around the overgrown garden. Mary pushed through the hanging bushels, releasing a potent scent of dried herbs, back out into the heavy rain and around to the back of the cottage.

'Podge! Podge Boylan could you not hear me calling you?'

There was no reply.

'This is no way to treat your first visitor in years, Podge Boylan!'

'Not the first' was all he said, as she came within a few steps of him. He was crouched at the stone, staring at it intently.

'Oh, no?' she asked, 'A steady stream of well-wishers, is it? Have you sobered up?'

Again, he was silent.

'Look, Podge, I need to talk to you about what you were saying in Greely's earlier. My boy, Sean, is missing. The guards are looking into it, but the last place he was seen was the MacCormacs' place in Rathlevean. You were saying something about them in the pub. I need to know what you were on about!'

'Look at this, would you?'

'Podge, I have no time for your quirks now, I …'

Sean's mother stopped when she noticed what Podge was pointing at. The face of the big grey stone was scored with a wide spiral groove. At the centre of the spiral was a small orange glow. It was lengthening too; moving along the gully slower than a snail.

'Is that some kind of glowworm, Podge? I'm not here to talk about insects, you know!'

'It's no worm.' He looked at her for the first time. 'Maura Sheridan, is it?'

'Mary, Podge. Mary.'

'Well, Mary Sheridan, it's no worm. It's happening on a few of these stones. It's happening at The Vale, too. The stones there were overgrown for years but someone has cleared them. And they have your "worms" crawling along their faces too. Just like the old song: "When the Old Stones, faced with spiral line, glow along those ancient scores …"!'

He started to cackle, and Mary lost all trace of patience. 'Where are the MacCormacs, Podge? And where is my boy?'

'By the looks of things, Mary, you'll know soon enough. We'll all know.'

Ayla had that feeling of whispered awe you sometimes get when you are in a huge church or a place of great natural beauty. A feeling of reverence, as if laughing or even just talking in it seemed vulgar, almost. From its dark little tunnels to its great vaulting arches, held up by the colossal statues of Maeve, this place was nightmarish, sure. But Ayla felt connected to it somehow. *I can't accept that the king and queen are my parents.*

But you can't help what you come from. Can you, dear?

She shrugged off the horrible feeling of the other voice and decided that they should return to the main chamber and continue down the giant steps. Ayla wasn't sure how she knew where to go; she just felt it somehow. She didn't speak to Finny, Benvy and Sean, lost as she was in a swirl of her own thoughts.

Ayla remembered a day in the Burren, when she had gone on a walk with her uncles across the limestone grykes to a place called Eagle Rock. She smiled at the memory of Fergus being nervous about a herd of bullocks – a man who could probably pick one up in each hand! Lann and Taig had taken the mickey out of him for days afterwards. On their way back the air was suddenly alive with electricity. Ayla could feel it in her hair, on her tongue. Then they had stood in silent awe as a barrage of pink fork lightning had erupted from a sudden swell of black clouds in the distance. It was the greatest show of nature Ayla had ever seen. And now she felt that same power coursing through her very veins. The tingling on her tongue was a hot sting. The lightning was in every cell of her slight form. It felt as if the clouds were writhing behind her eyes, charged by an energy that was powered by the sadness of her uncles' deaths. *The sadder I get*, she thought, *the stronger I feel*. Ayla shook herself out of the daydream, and concentrated on the path ahead.

All around them the yawning mouths of black windows stared down, following the gang as they walked. On every surface an ethereal blue light danced as the water of the lake rippled from an unfelt wind. The openings whistled with it. Each of the friends felt their hair ruffled and they noticed how their clothes flapped, but there was no real wind here to feel as such. It was like a ghost that danced among the bone-shaped pillars, warning them to retreat.

They were tired and hungry but never rested. Instead, Sean, Finny and Benvy talked amongst themselves as a distraction, while Ayla carried on silently, always a little ahead. The talking helped them to cope with the fear that, at any moment, the walls would swarm with goblins or one of the leviathan statues that hulked in the shadows would come to life and crush them. They reasoned that this was some kind of city for the goblins and their Red Root King and power-hungry queen. When they saw the balconied walls and the arena-style pit, they thought that the toad room must be there for entertainment; they could only imagine how many goblin-girls were sacrificed there for sport.

The three friends also spoke in hushed tones about Ayla and how she was acting. She was grieving, that was certain. They also worried that her new power was not having a good effect on their friend. None dared to ask: were they right in following her? What had seemed like a noble cause at the start, now seemed like the obsession of a girl who was clearly not herself. Finny said to the others that he'd speak to Ayla and see if he could help her out of whatever mental breakdown she was hurtling towards. If anyone could get through to her, it was him.

Though constantly on guard, nothing emerged to attack them. But they never caught sight of the lost goblin-girl either, despite wishing for her to appear. Benvy, in particular, hoped to see the little girl in the shadows, so that she could persuade her to join them.

The journey down the huge, wide steps that coiled up from the lake took a long time, until eventually they arrived at the edge of the eerie, blue water.

The first thing they noticed was that the surface of the lake was utterly still, like a sheet of pristine glass. Just under it, however, phosphorescence shuffled as if it was buffeted by the mysterious half-wind. The goblin city rose up high above them, and the water of the lake disappeared underneath the lowest balcony of arches into a deep cave.

'That's where we have to go.' It was the first time Ayla had spoken since the toads.

'Swimming again, I guess.' Benvy tried to sound brave, but the prospect frightened her.

Ayla stepped to the water's edge. It didn't lap to the shore of smooth rock; it remained utterly still until she moved to wade in, and then broad ripples fanned out from her submerged foot and moved lazily across the surface. The phosphorescence parted like glowing smoke. She was surprised to find that even after a few metres, it was only ankle deep. It was, however, bitingly cold. She carried on and, left with little choice, the friends followed her in, wordlessly.

They went slowly, ever-wary that the next step might plunge them deeper in to the icy water. They couldn't see the bottom through the spectral blue light, and so had no idea how deep it was. They also felt uncomfortably exposed now that they were surrounded by the vaulting city. But the depth remained a constant – just a few centimetres – and the group made their way across to the cave, without anything grabbing their ankles or hollering at them from the columned galleries, as much as they expected it to happen.

The cave was wide and its floor was thorny with stalagmites. They followed the water until the passage dropped down, suddenly steep. But where the water should have started to cascade, it only slumped. It acted more like a thick ooze than water, and the way was treacherously slippy. Sean was the first to lose his footing. With a loud *splosh* he was on his backside and barrelled through his friends, toppling them like skittles. They all hurtled down the passage, totally out of control, spinning like leaves on a torrent around wide bends and down sheer drops. At last, just as their speed reached a dizzying peak, they came to a gentle stop where the ground first rose gradually and then became level. The water gathered into another pool.

'Well, that was the first pain-free landing we've had so far!' chirped Sean. 'Sorry,' he added, when he saw the state of his now-soaked friends.

Looking around, the friends realised they were in another huge cavern, this one unadorned by hand but no less extravagant for it. They stared in wonder at the pockets of green and mauve algae illuminating the vast cavern. The ground undulated as if an ocean had been frozen in a moment. But the oddest sight of all was at its centre.

A circular lake shone still, its surface reflective like a mirror. It took a moment or two for the group to register that this was a reflection that they couldn't understand. The inverted scene was not of the ceiling of the cavern, as you would expect, but of another landscape: a line of tall conifer trees with the rolling tops of high hills and an azure, cloudless sky. It was, simply, not the right reflection of where they were now.

'Uh ...' Sean started, but couldn't think of what to say next.

The group picked their way along the flagstone floor to get a closer look. Finny lifted up a smooth rock. He tested its weight, and then flung it as hard as he could out over the lake. The rock landed with a definite splash, but did not cause a single ripple.

'Oookaaayyy …' Sean said. 'That is about the weirdest thing we've seen so far. And that's saying someth—'

He didn't get to finish his sentence because, like the others, he was becoming entranced by what was happening in the reflection. The clear sky had darkened and was filling quickly with banks of billowing, angry clouds. The trees had begun to sway, lazily at first, and then more violently. The cavern was also filling with a cold breeze that was escalating swiftly to a pounding, aggressive wind. Sean, Benvy and Finny had to hold each other for support. Ayla stood a few metres from them, strangely calm. Then they heard Finny shouting: 'Grab something! Run! Towards those columns! Quickly!'

Pulled this way and that by the jostling wind, they slipped and scurried over the rocks to a group of hourglass columns just as the clouds turned black and the first peel of thunder rumbled with menace.

'Ow!' What the *hell*?' shouted Benvy. Something had struck her painfully on the thigh. Then again on the arm. Something else exploded in shards of ice just centimetres from her head. It was tennis-ball-sized hailstones, being

flung *upwards* ferociously from the lake. The group huddled behind the rocky columns as another drum of thunder preceded the first of the lightning. This came in hot
spears up out of the lake, thrusting itself into the roof of
the cavern at every angle, causing huge chunks of stone to
fall. The wind screamed furiously through the cave. Finny,
Benvy and Sean could barely hold on.

Finny tried to shout, but the words were ripped away,
so he just pointed. Ayla was not with them. She was standing, stock still, by the edge of the lake. The storm appeared
to have no affect her; not even her hair was moving. Her
arms were raised, and they could see that her eyes were
alive with the sparking light again. She turned to them and
beckoned them over to her.

'What? Why is she doing this? She can't be *serious*?' Sean
shrieked, again unheard by anyone. Hailstones continued
to shoot straight up into the air from the surface of the
water in every direction, smashing into the ground by
their drenched and cold feet. There was no way they could
move. But still Ayla beckoned. Finny decided to make a
break for it.

CHAPTER 5

The Howling Night

In the cavern, the raging wind shoved Finny around mercilessly while hailstones now as big as footballs exploded around him. Each time he slipped, he was dragged further from Ayla, and every time he got up he was attacked again and again by the brutal gale. Still Ayla beckoned to him, calm and still. At last he reached her.

Sean and Benvy had also left the safety of cover. The hammer seemed unaffected by the wind and blazed defiantly blue. Both of them held on to it and together battled their way to their friends, using the weapon like an anchor in the hurricane. It was a slow, hard fight, but they reached Finny and he held on too. They were only inches from Ayla, but she was unruffled, as if standing in a different place altogether.

'Ayla!' Finny screamed over the tempest. 'What's happening? What do we do?'

When Ayla replied, she didn't need to raise her voice because it could be heard clearly above the raging storm, though the others had to shout to be heard against it. Her eyes were blindingly bright. 'We go through.'

She placed a hand on Finny, and in an instant he was unaffected by the winds. All was still.

'Take Benvy's hand. Benvy, take Sean's.'

They followed her instructions, and for them too the effects of the storm disappeared. Still around them it fulminated relentlessly.

'Come to the edge,' Ayla instructed them.

She knelt and dipped her face below the surface. Finny did the same. Instead of cold water, it was cold air he felt. He could breathe, smell the pines, hear the wind rushing through them. There was grass inches from his nose. Sean followed. They were not looking down to the depths of the lake, they were looking up into the sky. It was the strangest sensation; dipping their faces into cold water, only to emerge into cold air. They pushed themselves further in and found that they were hauling themselves out

on to the shores of a lake. There was no storm. The sky was blue as before. And there was no Benvy.

For just then, Benvy still on the other side of the lake, had spotted the goblin-girl, cowering behind a white curtain of drooping rock, close by the lake. Benvy called to the others, desperately trying to alert them, but Ayla and Finny had already disappeared into the water and Sean was halfway in. His hand was slipping from Benvy's. As soon as it was gone, Benvy found herself back in the throes of the violent and savage wind.

She realised she was still holding the hammer. She offered up a prayer of thanks that she had held on to it, and then she started the arduous haul over to where the little girl was crouching. By now the storm had reached fever pitch, insane and feral; Benvy was lifted off her feet, but somehow she managed to hold on, and the hammer succeeded in anchoring her. At last, she reached the girl. The poor child was screaming, though the storm ripped the sound away, and Benvy held the small figure tight to her chest. A brick of hailstones slammed into Benvy's legs causing her to howl in pain, but she gritted her teeth and turned, determined to make her way back to the edge of the lake. As Benvy struggled towards the water, with the girl hugged to her side, she noticed all had gone calm around them.

Ayla stood before her, her hand on her friend's shoulder. She walked with the two girls to the water's edge while, on all sides, boulders of ice shattered the cave walls and lightning writhed, filling the place with burning electricity. The three of them lowered themselves headfirst into the lake and emerged on the other side onto a grassy bank, blinking away the pain of daylight on their eyes and panting for breath in the crisp spring air.

Behind a line of tall evergreens the sky was beginning to redden, and the conifers made a long, slow whisper in the breeze. This place couldn't be more different from what Ayla, Sean, Benvy and Finny had left behind. It was the first taste of sweet, fresh air any of them had had in … how long, they couldn't remember. How long had they been down there in that underground hell? None of them could tell, and right now they didn't really care. They were just happy to be drinking in fresh air. Just for a while, they let themselves savour their new Alpine surroundings, running their hands through the cold, damp grass and lying on the soft clumps of the grassy bank, each to their own.

Before them, the bank of dark evergreen trees rose up on three sides from the grassy plains around the lake. Behind, the wide loch ended in a high, overhanging cliff which cast the waters of the lake half in shadow.

For a long time the goblin-girl wouldn't leave Benvy's

embrace. She clung tight, refusing to budge, burying her face into Benvy's filthy shirt. Benvy didn't mind. She held the younger girl, rocking her back and forth, telling her, over and over, that it was okay.

I will protect this girl no matter what, thought Benvy. *She's only little; not tough enough to survive on her own.*

'It's the light,' Ayla said.

'What is?' Benvy asked, and then realised. 'Oh!'

'She hasn't seen it in a long time. It's probably hurting her.'

Finny and Sean joined them.

'Is she alright?' Sean asked.

Still suspicious of the girl, Finny just snorted but it went unnoticed.

'I don't know to be honest,' said Benvy, 'I think so.'

'Well, she has you to thank, Benv'. You're mental. But you're brave too.' Sean smiled at his friend. 'She's going to need something more to wear other than those rags she has on. Here, take this.' He handed Benvy his hoody. 'It's baggy, so it should cover her.'

'Thanks.' Benvy pulled it over the girl's head; the child seemed puzzled but grateful nonetheless.

'Where are we, Ayla?' Finny asked.

'We're in Fal, I think. No, I *know* we are. I'm not sure how, but I know. Fal is still Ireland. Well, Ireland a long, long time ago.'

'So we might bump into Cuchulainn at some stage?'

Sean quipped. But nobody found this funny.

'What you did back there,' Finny continued, 'I mean, I know you had some new weird powers but *that* …? Why were you not blown out of it like the rest of us?'

'I'm not really sure. I kind of … zoned out. Like I was having a dream. A waking dream. But what I think is: that storm was there to stop Maeve and the Red Root King ever escaping. It was there to stop *anyone* ever coming to Fal. Somehow though Maeve must have gone through. I think she is ahead of us. But for me it felt like it was there to … sort of *welcome* me. I don't know. I don't know about anything. I really need to … '

With that, Ayla dropped to the ground in a faint.

'Ayla!' Sean and Finny ran to her side – thankfully she was still breathing. She had just passed out, probably from sheer exhaustion. She lay so still and looked like she was in a deep sleep.

Benvy and the girl were stretched out on the grass too; sleep was claiming them, though Benvy tried to stay awake. Between them, the boys carried Ayla over and carefully laid her on the grass beside the others.

'I'm not really tired, are you?' asked Finny.

'Nah. Too much going on in my head to sleep,' Sean replied.

'How about we go and explore the place to try and get our bearings?'

Sean agreed, once they could keep within a safe distance of their sleeping friends, and the two fetched their weapons, just in case.

The first thing they noticed was the sheer size of everything. They were getting used to feeling small, having come from the vast goblin city, but when they had first emerged here they had been too confused to take in the scale of their new surroundings. Now, as they walked through the stiff grass towards the conifer forest they could see that everything here was a grander proportion than normal too. The fir trees were not that close; it just seemed as if they were because they were so *huge*. Behind the treetops, mountains of bracken and gorse hulked, their backs disappearing high into the encroaching night.

The boys stopped to climb up on to an enormous rock for a better vantage point and each allowed their eyes to follow the bank of trees in opposite directions to look for a gap. There was none, and they looked back in the direction of the lake to check on their friends

'Holy God ... What's *that*?'

Behind the cliff, a conical mountain with near-vertical sides rose into the blue sky. It was as if the foot of the mountain had been scooped away to form the pale, sheer face of the escarpment. Perched on top of the cliff was an immense statue of a man. The figure was hooded and kneeling on one leg, with a flowing cloak that gathered in gigantic piles around it. One hand rested on a knee, while the other held a hammer that looked just like the one Sean had. Under his cowl, the statue's face was grim and stared down upon the lake with eternal, unbreakable intent. From its forehead, two huge stag horns forked out into the sky. Between them, carved into the forehead, was a spiral.

'Ho ... ly ... *God*,' said Sean again.

The boys stared at the statue for a long time before jumping down off the rock and making their way to the nearest of the trees. When they got to them, they found that the forest was practically impenetrable. At every point they tried to push in, but the way was blocked by a dense web of branches as strong as any brick wall. They decided to head back to the lake and tell the others what they'd found.

Finny couldn't contain the nagging feeling he had been having since they saved the goblin. 'Hey, Sean. The girl. What if she's still ... y'know ... one of them? She might not look like one anymore, but do you think we can really trust her?'

'Ah, Finny. She's just a kid! You can see how scared she is. I think we're safe. Well, relatively safe, given we have just come through an underground, black–magic hell to emerge into a potentially deadly ancient Ireland, on a quest led by a friend who can now pull storms out of thin air.'

'Yeah,' Finny had to laugh a little at Sean's humour. 'I suppose. There's another thing, though. Not the girl. Something else that's bothering me. I don't want to freak you out.'

'Just by saying that, you've freaked me out, Finny.'

'Sorry. It's just. Do you get the feeling we're being watched? And I don't mean by *him*.' He nodded to the statue.

'Yeah! But to be honest I've had it since this whole thing started, pretty much.'

'No, I mean …'

Their conversation was interrupted by a long, loud howl.

Finny and Sean looked at each other for a second and then ran as quickly as their legs could carry them back to the girls. The sound had woken Ayla and Benvy and they were up and on their feet by the time their friends reached them. They were relieved to see the boys.

Benvy was looking around frantically. But then she realised the little girl was gone again.

'Where *is* she?' Benvy asked the others.

But there was no sign of her. And they had no time to look as, once more, the evening sky was filled with howling. This time it came from more than one source.

'We need to get out of here fast and find some cover! That sounds like wolves to me!' Finny pointed towards the cliff. 'We need to find a way up there. We can look for somewhere to hide by the statue.'

'Statue? What statue?' Benvy asked.

'You'll see. Come on, we have to go!' said Sean urgently.

'Wait! I'm not leaving her again! You guys go, I'll catch up!' Benvy picked up her javelin and looked around, trying to decide where a little girl might head off to in a wooded wilderness.

'Hang on, Benvy!' Sean pleaded. 'You're no good to her dead, are you? We need to get up there, where it's high up and, hopefully, safe. Then we can try and spot her. To be honest, she's probably up there anyway. There's nowhere else she could have gone. There's no way through those trees, even for a small person.'

Benvy struggled with her conscience before deciding that Sean was right.

'Let's get up there and try and spot her. As soon as we do, we will go and get her. Wolf or no wolf!'

They all agreed and skirted the lake as quickly as they could and followed it until they reached the scree slope of the pale limestone mountain. The forest ended and the slope climbed gradually up to the peak. In front of the mountain a cliff jutted out and the girls had their first glimpse of the enormous hooded figure of the sentinel statue. There was another howl, a distance away but still too close. The friends scrambled up the loose rocks as fast as they could but the going was difficult. At certain points the only way was scarily close to the cliff edge. The fall would take them down to the waters of the lake, but God only knew where that would lead. At this height anyway, water lost its cushioning properties. In the pink dusk light, they rounded the giant pillar of the huge statue's hammer and reached the great swathes of its cloak and the protruding foot.

There was no warning bark or long howl this time. It was the sound of sliding rocks that gave the wolf away. It was grungy, slate grey with hateful yellow eyes. The beast picked its way carefully up the slope, a pink tongue dangling between long white fangs. Its eyes never left them, even when it slipped. From the trees behind, two more wolves emerged.

'Get up there!' Finny shouted. He bent and took Ayla's foot in his cupped hands, hoisting her up onto the big toe of the stone statue. She could just about reach with Finny holding her as high as his burning arms would go. Sean made to do the same for Benvy, but she raised an eyebrow and linked her hands for him. He struggled too, but managed it and hauled her up as Finny boosted her from below. Finny was the last.

The wolf had arrived quicker than they had expected and was now only a few metres away. They could hear its snuffling breath. It was much bigger than your ordinary wolf. With his back to the statue, Finny held up his sword and made ready to fight. By now, the other two wolves had arrived.

'Finny, get up here!' his friends shouted down to him frantically. Making a last minute decision, Finny only just had enough time to take a few steps away from the statue, turn and take a short run, and leap as high as he could for their outstretched arms. They managed to catch hold of him and hauled him up – just as the biggest wolf pounced with slavering, snapping jaws, missing the boy's ankles by millimetres.

'I don't think they can get at us down there,' said Sean, pointing down to the other side of the statue, the shape of which was making a natural enclosure.

With hearts pounding, the four friends lowered them-selves down the other side of the statue's foot and found, as they'd hoped, that it was protected from the outside. They were safe for now, the far end of the enclosure cut off by the giant statue's bended knee. To the right lay the cliff edge and to the left the cloak of the statue rose up fifty metres into the sky. It would be the perfect place to camp, though they were not completely sure the wolves or something else would not find its way in.

'If we can get over, I'd be very surprised if those wolves can't,' Sean voiced what they were all thinking. 'We're going to have to do something!'

As if on cue, they heard the growls just on the other side of the gigantic foot. Then the ominous sound of claw on stone as the beasts tried their best to scale it.

'Right,' said Benvy. 'I'm going to fling my flippin' javelin at the first ugly mutt to stick its head over there!'

Sean readied his hammer. 'Ayla? Any chance of a fork or two of lightning?' he asked. But Ayla was staring out over the cliff edge. 'I hope she's getting herself "in the zone",' he mumbled to himself.

Finny picked his sword up and the three approached the foot, ready to hoist each other up and do battle. Then before they could climb back up onto the statue, a large snout with lips curled and teeth bared poked over the stone. With that, in a single bound, a wolf was atop the foot. It licked its lips with its long, slimy tongue, and Sean, Benvy and Finny could see that it was ready to pounce. At the very last second something struck it on the head, its eyes widened and it fell back, dead. Then there was a yelp from the other side and the *flump* of another heavy body hitting the ground. The friends stopped in their tracks, confused. The last remaining wolf let out a long howl. There was a whistle in the air, a *flump* and the howl was cut out. Then there was silence.

They waited for a long time, but all was still.

'Give me a leg up,' said Finny finally.

He pulled himself up and slowly moved to look over

the other side of the statue, sword at the ready.

'Huh?' was all he said, relaxing.

'Well? What is it?' Sean asked impatiently.

'Get me up there,' Benvy said to Sean, grabbing him by the arm.

'Eh. Well,' Finny called down to them. 'The wolves are all dead.'

'What? How?' Both Sean and Benvy were firing questions up at Finny.

'Not sure. There's blood on their heads. Looks like they were hit with something. And, uh … That's not all.'

'Sheridan, get me up there, for God's sake!' Benvy was really losing patience.

Sean helped her up, and she in turn pulled him up onto the foot.

Together they saw the dead wolves. And there standing among them was the girl.

CHAPTER 6

The Pillars of The Danann

As night set in, the little group of friends decided to stay in the relative shelter of the statue. The fire they had lit, courtesy of a spark from Ayla's eyes on some dry twigs from a dead gorse bush, had gone from flame to ember, and the night arrived with a billion stars, reflected in the lake two hundred metres below them.

Earlier, with the fire sorted, they at last had time to think. But soon the talking turned to bickering. Now their arguing had gotten past the point of no return. There was nothing Sean or Finny could say, and anything they tried was either shot down or ignored by Ayla and Benvy. The girls were too lost in the fight with each other to pay attention to the boys.

Sean braved it again. 'Benvy's right, though, Ayla. You must know she's right!'

Ayla's eyes blitzed again, her vexation growing.

'There is no "right", Sean! There is only Maeve! If she isn't stopped then everything is over! Can you not understand that?'

'Don't threaten us with that sparky-eye *crap*, Ayla!' Benvy's voice echoed around the hollow behind the statue's leg. The little girl was clinging to Benvy, hiding behind her back as she had done since they pulled her over the giant statue's foot to rejoin their group.

Ayla groaned. 'I'm not *threatening* you, Benvy! I'm asking you! Trust me!'

Finny tried to interject but was overshot by Benvy for the thousandth time.

'Trusting you has not been great for us so far, has it?'

'Ah, Benvy ... That's going too far,' Finny said.

'*No*! Look where it's gotten us! Further from home, battered and bruised and nearly eaten by wolves! And anyway, it's not even the point! The point *is*: our only reason for risking our lives here, *apparently*, was so that we could return some of those poor creatures in the tunnels to human form and get them home. Well, we have managed

to save *one*. And getting her home is what we have to do now. End of.'

'But we don't know anything about her, Benvy!' Finny replied, avoiding looking at the little face peering round Benvy's side. 'She could still be one of the queen's nasty, little helpers? Maybe, just *maybe*, she's the reason Ayla's been acting so weird? Sorry, Ayls, but you have been.'

Ayla's expression didn't change. She knew she had been acting strangely. She just couldn't help it. *Finny you are my closest friend in the whole world. But I couldn't even begin to tell you what's going on inside me now. I'm not even sure myself. But you wouldn't understand anyway, would you? Useless, pithy boy.*

'I think that girl is part of the problem,' Finny said, folding his arms. 'She just killed three giant wolves! She could probably kill us too – if we aren't careful.'

Benvy only just resisted the urge to punch Finny. 'Once again, Oscar Finnegan, your fear of a tiny little girl shows your true colours. A waster is what you are. It's what you always have been. And Ayla was acting weird long before we found this little girl. Stop trying to defend her all the time. Your sucking-up is pathetic!'

For a second Finny was shocked by this out-and-out attack, and then anger turned his cheeks hot. 'And what about you? You're just looking for a little doll whose hair you can brush so you can pretend to be a girl for once?'

'Whoa there, calm down everyone,' Sean leapt between

them before they could get physical. 'There's no point lashing out here.'

Benvy stormed off to the far side of the hollow, the little girl stumbling to keep up. Ayla went in the opposite direction, to sit at the edge of the cliff and seethe. Finny and Sean were left by the fire. They didn't talk, just exchanged knowing, worried looks and prodded the fire with sticks.

Eventually, after an hour or more of silence, each of them settled themselves into uncomfortable sleep. Later, when a huge full moon hung in the cloudless night, Finny stirred. It wasn't a noise that woke him. It was a sense. Something in him, a dream maybe, jolted him from sleep. He looked around. Sean was snoring lightly at his feet. Benvy and the girl had made their way back to the warmth of the fire and were lying huddled together, asleep. He could barely look at them. Someone had had the foresight to put another stick on the fire and it crackled hungrily. There was no sign of Ayla.

Finny sat up and glanced around, giving his eyes a minute to get used to the darkness so that he could just about see most of the hollow in the dim light. Ayla definitely wasn't where he had last seen her, staring out from the cliff edge. He got up as quietly as he could, knowing the truth of the situation: she was gone.

As Finny prepared himself to climb up out over the huge foot to go in search of Ayla, he looked back at the sleeping silhouettes of Sean, Benvy and the girl. He already had his sword and a slab of toad-meat in his hands. He had picked them up as soon as his eyes had opened. He stuffed the meat into his trouser pocket and with a short run-up, he jumped and caught the top of the statue's foot and pulled himself up and over.

On the other side, he immediately spotted Ayla in the distance, clambering along the steep flank of the mountain. In another few minutes she would have disappeared behind the line of evergreens.

'This is the way it has to be guys,' he whispered, and set off after Ayla.

Sean, Benvy and the little girl were sitting silently in the cold dawn. They had woken a while before to find that both Finny and Ayla were missing, and so they were waiting, hoping their friends would return, maybe with firewood or food, or even both. Sean hoped that with a bit of warmth and some grub the tension between them all would fade and they could find a solution to the awkward stand-off. The three waited for a long time.

Finally the waiting turned to worry. Maybe Finny and Ayla had come up against wolves again – or something worse. They could be out there hurt. But maybe … maybe there was another reason for their disappearance. It was too much of a coincidence: the worst argument they had ever had, and now they were gone.

The sun had crept up a little higher, bringing with it a small but welcome bit of heat. On the horizon a bank of clouds gathered, dark and heavy. They could smell the rain in the air. Slowly, intensely, fury bubbled up in Benvy. In Sean, his feeling was more one of sickening despondency. The fight had torn them apart, he realised now; their friends had left them to pursue their own goals.

The first fat drops of rain fell sporadically and then burst all at once into a drenching veil. Benvy screamed into the sky, kicking the grass and flinging stones out over the edge of the cliff. Sean just sat, with his head in his hands. The little girl watched from the cowls of the giant statue, frightened and confused. Fury vented, Benvy stopped at last and slumped to the ground beside Sean, letting her head rest for a minute on his shoulder.

'We're going to have to go, Benv',' Sean said.

'Yep' was all she said in reply.

'Any thoughts on where?'

'Nope.'

After a time the rain subsided at least. Sean walked over to the cliff edge and scanned the landscape as best he could. The view was awash with mist, sodden with earthy colours of brown and grey and bottle-green. Beyond the jagged canopy of trees, mountains breached the fog, rolling their bracken-covered backs like leviathan whales in a sea of pines. In the valley between them, way off on the horizon, something caught Sean's eye. *Hang on a sec.* He thought. *Surely that can't be right?* It looked for all the world like a hazy city of skyscrapers.

He covered the eye on the side of his glasses with the missing lens and strained to get a better look through the remaining lens, but he still couldn't trust his sight. The shapes looked like the tall buildings of an American city, but they seemed crooked, like tall, skinny, old men with bad backs. They were very dim in the grey fog. He called Benvy over.

'Benvy! Come here and have a look at this, will you?'

There was no answer.

'Benvy! Come on! I think there's … something. A city? I dunno, I'm …'

'Half-blind? No kidding.' Benvy stood beside him, ordering the girl to stay back from the ledge with a stern finger. She let out a long sigh. Sean could see bags of dark tiredness gathered below her brown eyes. She looked a bit gaunt and very pale, even for her.

'Are you okay, Benv'?' he asked, concerned no longer with the towers, but with his friend's well-being. She had always been so strong – so much stronger than him.

However, with all that was happening, he had seen cracks appear. Cracks that he worried would split her apart. He was sick that Ayla and Finny had left them alone here.

'I'm grand. What is it I'm supposed to be seeing?'

He pointed beyond the forest to the deep valley.

'Keep following the valley. Right at the end there. Poking out from the mist.'

She squinted.

'It's like skyscrapers? Oh, God, please tell me we're in America or somewhere and this is all just a nightmare.' She wasn't joking. Sean was sorry he couldn't say *yes*.

'I wish' was all he could say. 'I don't know what it is. But given what we've seen in the last while …' He paused as he realised that he had no idea how long they'd been away from home. '… eh, given what we've seen, my guess is it's going to have some kind of magic about it. And in my book, that seems to be the best place to start. With getting our new friend home, I mean.'

'I miss *our* home, Sheridan.'

'I know. Me too.'

It was the middle of Saturday night and the blocky buildings of Finny's all-boys school, St Augustin's, hulked as shadows in the moonlight. The walls were feathered with

123

ivy that bristled as the wind passed through the leaves. Down in the bowels of the oldest building, Fr Shanlon, the school's feared principal, and Finny's one-time sparring partner (known not-quite-affectionately as 'The Streak'), sat utterly still in the only chair in his sparse quarters. He had been sitting in this slumped pose for a very, very long time for he was deeply troubled.

He hadn't eaten, or slept (he never did, really) in all of that time. His green, bloodshot eyes stared straight ahead behind his thick glasses, and nothing stirred except his breathing, which was glacially slow. And then, suddenly, he jerked upright and gasped for breath as if he had been holding it all that time. He looked around, confused for a second, and then stared down at his fingers. He struggled to free his stiff hands from the arms of the chair as his nails were almost sunk into the wood. He loosened his clawlike grip, and stood up. He took a key from the roof of his mouth, his own unique and peculiar hiding place, and unlocked the heavy door facing the main entrance to his room, a door that had only been opened once in more than a thousand years.

It was here that Fr Shanlon had brought Ayla's three giant uncles – Lann, Fergus and Taig MacCormac – to commune with the Old Ones: an ancient council of which he was a member. The door led to a cavern as old as Ireland itself, and in this cavern were pillars lined with ogham script. Fr Shanlon was able to use this secret place to make contact with the other members of his order. For Fr Shanlon was not really Fr Shanlon. He was Cathbad, a Druid of Fal, and he was six thousand years old almost to the year.

Moonlight hung from a cavity in the high, dripping ceiling of the inner chamber. The light fell onto a still pool at the centre and wavered slowly along the great ogham-etched columns that framed the chamber.

Cathbad threw down his glasses, stepped into the water and waded to the middle. The beam of light sprang to life, fractured by the rippling water and sent to every corner in jittering strands like electricity. The druid began his chant, as the beam was severed by a single cloud and the cavern plunged into darkness.

As the chant grew in intensity, a dim unearthly blue glow appeared above the tallest column and brightened until a phantom face was revealed. The disembodied face spoke:

'*Cathbad, what news?*'

The druid raised his head, his eyes now ablaze with bright, smoky light.

'Midir, I am deeply troubled.'

'*As are we all, Earth-Brother.*'

'I have searched in the dark. I have found only darkness.'

Silence.

'Why is my sight so dimmed?'

'We are all blind now, Cathbad. Maeve, our Lost Sister, has returned. She covers our eyes with a cold hand.'

'It is as I feared. And what of the girl? What of Ayla?'

'She runs to her.'

'Then it is time for me to return also. I need you to open the gate near the White Hill.'

'As you wish, Cathbad. Proceed with care. Maeve grows in power.' With those parting words, Midir's phantom face vanished.

Then Cathbad left the cavern, locking the door behind him. He returned the key to its hiding place in the roof of his mouth and made his way out of the school. He walked through the night in great strides, across fields and rivers to Sheedys' farm close to Knockwhite hill, lighting his way with otherworldy, glowing green eyes.

Back in the realms of Fal, Sean, Benvy and the goblin-girl had descended the slope and had almost reached the dense treeline. They had made sure to keep low and out of sight as much as possible. Of course they knew this was point-less against the keen nose of a wolf, but it was all they could do. Their feelings were mixed about entering the forest. On the one hand, the evergreens' cover would be welcome. On the other, God only knew what was waiting for them in there. As it happened, they struggled even to find a way in.

'I told you, me and Finny couldn't find a way in anywhere,' said Sean. 'We should have looked for a way around.'

'Mention *his* name again ...' Benvy threatened, 'and I'll punch you. A way *around* would have been miles and miles in the wrong direction. We'll find a gap. We just need to keep looking.'

Their clothes and skin were suffering numerous tears from the serpentine branches and brambles that blocked the way. Sean received another nasty scratch, close to where the cut on his hip had reopened and it stung painfully.

'*Argh*! This is *hopeless*!' He raised up the hammer in fury and swung it at the thicket. It simply snagged and refused to come out easily, goading his frustration. Benvy smiled for the first time in ages. Then her smile dropped away.

'Hang on, where ... Ah *no*! Not *again*! she shouted. 'Where has she gone this time?'

Sean pointed. 'She's there.'

The girl was indeed just nearby and she was calling them over. She had found a small gap in the undergrowth. It formed a green tunnel, just wide enough to crawl through.

'Ha! Nice one, little girl!' Benvy said and laughed.

Sean threw his eyes to heaven. 'Brilliant, just what we need. More crawling.'

After twenty minutes of wriggling down the verdurous tunnel, they emerged onto soft ground swathed in pine needles. The red-barked evergreens went on and on until they disappeared into muffled darkness. There was no birdsong, no rustling wind and barely any light. Each tree was barbed with rapier-like branches from top to bottom and in every direction.

The tunnel had been almost perfectly straight, and roughly in the direction of the mountains.

'Straight ahead, so. No turns, no veering,' Benvy said, as if it was going to be easy.

'Simple,' Sean said with unhidden sarcasm. 'But first I think I need to do something about this.'

He peeled away his shirt and jeans tentatively to reveal the cut on his side, widened and sodden with blood.

'Oh, God, Sheridan!' Benvy gasped.

'Yeah, it's a bit agonisingly painful alright,' he said, breathlessly.

The girl tugged at his elbow. She held up a finger as if to say: *wait*. Then down: *sit*. She disappeared into the gloom, leaving Benvy confused as to who she should protect. In the end, she stayed with Sean, silently praying that the girl would return. After a short time, she did.

She held a large pine cone in her hands. Handing it

to Benvy, she gestured at her to break it in half. With a bit of effort, it cracked. A thick, sticky syrup oozed out of the centre. The girl dipped a finger in and applied the viscous sap to the wound in Sean's side as gently as she could. Then she handed Sean a twig and snapped her teeth together. *Bite.* Sean gave her a worried look, but complied. The girl then pinched the two sides of the wound together in a fearsome grip, holding the flesh relentlessly tight. Sean screamed long and loud, but his scream was muffled by the dense, uncaring forest.

When Sean had recovered, they continued on. The wound felt different, Sean realised. The worst of the pain was a fading memory. Whatever the girl had done, she had helped seal his torn flesh. Ahead of him Sean watched her picking her way deftly through the mesh of tree trunks, never snagging on a branch or pausing for a rest. Barely any light found its way to the forest floor, and Sean was sure that the shadows held unimaginable horrors. It certainly felt like they were unwelcome there, in the quiet. But the girl seemed almost happy for once.

Struggling to keep up, Benvy and Sean were glad to see some life return to their young charge, and her new positivity eased the sense of dread the two friends were feeling. Just watching the girl revel in this environment served as a distraction from the pain of Ayla and Finny's betrayal.

'She seems happy in the woods,' Sean said to Benvy, when they had paused for a moment's rest.

'Yeah, I know what you mean. She reminds me of you when you get your head stuck in a new book. The sight of you in a library – it's like watching an animal released into the wild. Wait, where's she going *this* time?'

As the friends watched, the small girl skipped up a tree as easily as if it was a regular staircase and vanished into the canopy.

After a minute, she returned, descending a different trunk entirely. In her hand she held three small blue eggs. She cracked one against the bark and drank the innards, offering the others to her rescuers.

Sean and Benvy took them reluctantly at first, concerned that they might belong to some pretty songbird or, God forbid, contain cute little chicks close to hatching. But their stomachs were protesting and, in the end, they ate them hungrily.

The girl pointed into the gloom; it was obvious enough that she was pointing the way to go.

'She must have had a look when she was up there. Clever girl!' Benvy gave her the thumbs-up. The girl seemed chuffed.

A little further on, they were delighted to find that the space between the trees broadened, and the going became easier. The dense evergreens gave way to deciduous oaks and beech, and late-afternoon light found its welcome way into the wood. At last, they arrived at the edge of the forest and the way to reach the mountains beyond. Up close the mountain slopes were even more beautiful, a painter's palette of yellow gorse, mauve grasses and white limestone. Threads of silver rivulets forked down their sides like forks of lightning. In the middle was a wide, boggy valley with tufts of tall, yellow grass and pools of brown peat-water. The travellers welcomed the open space again and sank to their knees to drink from a nearby icy stream.

Re-energised, they walked on. Benvy tried to talk to the girl again. 'Name,' she said, pointing to her own chest. 'Benvy. My … name … is Benvy.' Then she pointed at the girl who just looked at blankly back at her.

'Ach, I give up,' grumbled Benvy.

Just then, the girl stopped. She placed a hand on herself, and said clearly, 'Ida.'

'Ida? Ee-da? Hey! Your name is Ida? Me, Ben-vee. You, Ida?'

The girl smiled, and the two laughed together.

After a couple of hours of picking their way among the muddy pools on the valley floor, they had almost passed through the mountains. Ahead, closer than they had imagined, loomed the great towers they had seen from the statue's cliff top. The shapes were not buildings, though, but a stand of immense columns of stone. Thrusting a hundred metres into the sky, their crooked corners were scarred with deep grooves. They were ogham stones, but on a huge scale. Although the sky had cleared and the evening was fresh, the feet of the pillars remained hidden in a soupy shroud of mist.

The Constant Shadow

Finny had followed Ayla at a safe distance for hours. They were, by now, about ten kilometres away from the statue and their friends. Finny thought he would be better off hanging back, in order to keep a better eye on Ayla and spot any potential danger. He was also afraid she would force him to leave, sending him back to Benvy and Sean and the little girl. He couldn't let that happen. He had to protect Ayla at all costs. She was the closest person in the world to him. When his life spiralled out of control, it was Ayla who stopped the spinning. And

anyway, Finny wasn't sure he could be around Benvy Caddock anymore.

They're idiots for trusting that little goblin-girl, he thought. *They've made their bed and that's that.* But really he wished they hadn't fought, and he felt especially bad that he had left Sean who had, as ever, done nothing wrong.

They had skirted the steep mountainside for a couple of hours, keeping the bank of trees on their left and following the rough ground to the right. By late morning, they had rounded the mountain and were high enough to be able to see the land that lay behind the peak. Finny was surprised to find that beyond the rocky plains, a distant ocean stretched out as still as concrete.

As they walked, a persistent sense that they were being watched troubled him. The fear that at any moment another horse-sized wolf might burst from the treeline was ever-present, but this felt like something else.

On numerous occasions he was sure he saw a movement in the undergrowth – a shadow too small to be a wolf, too big to be a bird and all too fleeting to guess what else it might be. Finny watched the forest to catch it again, but never succeeded. It happened again and again just in the corner of his eye as the sun arced across the clear sky. He was also wary that Ayla would suddenly turn around and spot him, so he ensured that he always stayed a safe distance back.

By midday, Ayla had stopped on the bank of a narrow river. Hiding behind a slab of limestone, Finny watched her drink. He took his chunk of toad from his pocket, by now the meat was close to going really bad, but Finny ate it anyway, ignoring his stomach's urge to reject the slimy flesh. He followed his thoughts as they drifted from Ayla to his friends and to all that had happened, and then home. Everything he knew had been upended, flung around, and, in all truth, torn asunder by circumstances that had no basis in reality. He wasn't particularly happy in his old life, but it was a life, at least. And back there in it, he wondered if his mother and father had gone to the police, if the whole of Kilnabracka or even the whole of Munster were out looking for him and his friends. He wondered if, in some strange self-sacrificial twist, his disappearance had brought his parents together again, united in grief. Or maybe they didn't grieve at all.

If I do make it home, he thought, *how will I ever tell them about this? And what about Benvy and Sean. How will I tell their families that I left them alone in a dangerous place while they slept?*

But if Ayla was to be believed then none of that really mattered unless she achieved her goals. *The things I've seen her do …* Ayla was special, there was no doubt about it. And this was real. Ayla needed help to succeed, and if that cost everything then so be it.

137

Finny decided now was the time to make himself known to her. *She might even be glad to see me.* He stood up, and in that instance saw a dark figure creeping among the bracken towards his friend.

Like on the sports field, Finny didn't think, he just reacted. He sprinted down the slope, leaping over rocks and grykes, hollering as loud as he could with his sword held up, ready to strike.

The shadow saw him and changed direction to run to meet him. Hearing their approach behind her, Ayla had jumped up in fright and shouted, '*Finny!*'

Up close, Finny could see the figure in detail. It was a boy, a little older and taller than him. He looked like some kind of native warrior, clothed only in a sort of kilt, his knotty muscles daubed with painted spirals. His hair was shaved into a mohawk and on his face he had the beginnings of a light, wispy beard. His eyes were wide and wild.

He pounced up to meet Finny in long, agile leaps and before Finny could even swing his blade – the warrior had ducked, thrusting a shoulder into Finny's chest, flipping him high into the air. With a crunch, Finny landed painfully onto a flat rock, gasping for breath. The warrior boy then turned and dived on Finny, wrapping his legs around his waist and his hard arms around his neck. Finny's throat was clamped shut; his ribs creaked as if they were squeezed to breaking point.

By this time, Ayla had reached them. Her eyes were on fire.

'Let … go … of … him,' she ordered, as a single cloud started to swirl above her head.

The warrior's grip relaxed, and he rolled off his opponent's back. It took a moment for Finny's windpipe to open again and suck up air in hoarse gasps. Ayla helped him up. 'Oh, my God! Are you okay?'

'M … My sword!' he choked. 'Ayla get … back.' He was trying to get to his feet and push Ayla away.

The rangy warrior-boy laughed, and danced on the spot, throwing jabs into the air. He strutted around, puffing his chest out and flicking his feet in front of him like some kind of over-confident rooster. All the while he was grinning.

'Shhh. It's okay, I can handle him.' Ayla instructed Finny, 'You sit for a minute.' She looked up at the prancing warrior-boy. 'Who the hell are you? I'm warning you, don't even think about attacking us again, or I'll fry you on the spot!'

The young warrior replied in a language that Finny couldn't understand. To his surprise, Ayla seemed to understand him perfectly and she even replied in kind. The words sounded quite a bit like Irish.

Ayla translated. 'He says his name is Lorcan. He's here to fetch me and take me somewhere.'

Then she seemed to register Finny's presence properly.

'What the hell are *you* doing here anyway?' She was trying to sound angry, but it was clear that she was actually glad Finny had followed her.

Glancing between the two of them, Lorcan said something else.

Again Ayla translated. 'He said something along the lines of: "Fair play to you for trying …".' She asked Lorcan to repeat something, 'What was the last word again? Ah … Uh … "Fair play to you for trying … horse-arse."' Ayla couldn't help it. She found herself grinning. Finny did not smile back.

'How can you understand that? It's not Irish, is it?'

'It is! Or at least it's the language that Irish comes from. And how do I know it? I've no idea. Just another one of those things.'

'Well, you might ask him why we should trust him. And also, please tell him from me, if I'm the horse's arse, he's what comes out of it.'

Ayla and Lorcan spoke some more.

'He says it was him who killed those wolves back at the statue.'

To demonstrate, Lorcan produced a leather sling, put a rock in it, and spun it so fast the sling became a blur. All the time he held eye-contact with Finny, with the corner of his mouth turned up in smugness. Finny had never wanted to punch someone so much in all his life.

So it wasn't the goblin-girl.

'Finny, I'm sorry about this. He's a bit of a doofus. But I need his help and I'm only translating.'

'Yeah, yeah. I know.'

'He also says you should be grateful he didn't do the same to you when he saw you following me. He watched us all arguing and wasn't sure if we were friends. But he was told to bring me and whoever was with me to … Where was it?'

Lorcan answered.

'He's bringing us to people who can help us. They'll help us find Maeve, Finny!'

'And you believe him? You think we can trust him?' Finny had struggled gingerly to his feet, trying to shrug off the pain in his ribs and pretend he was fine but he couldn't hide a wince.

'Hey! Give that back!' he yelled as Lorcan moved forward swiftly and scooped up his sword. Lorcan ignored him, inspecting the weapon with a look of approval. He spun it around in his hands – just as quickly as the sling, over and back, propeller-fast. He finished with some lunges for effect, and offered it back to Finny, handle-first. Impatiently, Finny took the sword and performed his own little twirl, but Ayla and their strange new companion had turned their backs and were headed to the riverbank.

Sean's mother, Mary Sheridan, had tried calling both the garda station and home numerous times, but there was no signal out in the deep countryside and the tone went dead each time. She could only pray that they had some new information.

In the meantime, she had made the decision to head out to where Ayla's uncles, the MacCormac brothers, had been working before they disappeared. She drove as fast as she could to Sheedys' farmhouse without careening off the road into a ditch. It was early on Sunday morning, and the beginnings of daylight had peered over the horizon. She had spent a sleepless night at home, and then was up and gone in the early hours to collect Podge Boylan from the edge of Coleman's Woods. Mary suspected Podge knew more than he was letting on. The old man was silent in the car. He insisted on having the window down, despite the rain, and he stared out into the dawn. Sean's mother was by now fully sick of the old man's peculiar nature, but something told her to follow his story to its conclusion, for want of a better lead. There was no denying the trail of light she had seen on the stones (though she decided not to tell her husband about it, not yet), and part of her was not entirely dismissive of otherworldly happenings. She had her own experience of them, of a kind.

There had been an incident in her childhood that she had never spoken about, not even to Jim. In fact, her brain had done a good job of burying the event entirely – a repressed memory which now, given its new relevance, started to seep back into her consciousness.

She had been about Sean's age, and she had run away after a fight with her own mother, over what she had no idea now. She had just left through the back door without packing a bag and made straight for Coleman's Woods, swearing never to return. She would live in the woods, on her own, forever, and they would never find her.

Mary had been found after a full thirty hours, freezing cold and starving. Her mother had been beside herself, unsure of whether to hug her child or spank the behind off her and had chosen the latter. But young Mary had been unable to talk for days after it. She had been so frightened by something she had seen in the woods, near the clearing. Something that had happened …

Out there, in the woods, something had appeared out of the darkness and grabbed hold of her – a hand. Or more like a claw. It had black skin blacker than tar. And horrible long fingers. And the eyes …

She remembered how she had fought and kicked and screamed until the thing had let go for just long enough for her to run and run and run …

The memory caused old fears to rise up all over again; Mary sniffed back a tear, suddenly aware that she had not been concentrating properly on the road.

Podge was staring at her, not saying anything, but he looked almost sympathetic.

Mary cleared her throat. '*Ahem*. So. We're nearly at Sheedys', Podge. Please tell me we'll find something there that will lead to my boy.'

'We'll find something, Mary. I don't know what yet.'

'This is all too much.'

Tears brimmed again. Sean's mother sucked in a deep breath, determined to keep it together. *You're doing the right thing, Mary. The guard is following up the MacCormacs. Jim is at home by the phone. This is your only option.*

Podge interrupted her thoughts. 'You were that girl, the one who ran away. And was in the woods for a day or two. Am I right?'

Mary slowed down, and looked at the old man.

'How did you know about that?'

'Sure, I was one of the folk out looking for you. I know those woods better than any man. It was me who spotted you first!'

She didn't know what to say.

'I had a daughter too, once,' he announced solemnly.

'You what?' Mary couldn't believe it. Podge had always been alone – as far as she could remember.

'I had a daughter. And a son too. He's in Dublin these days. Nearly an old man himself at this stage. Doesn't come home much, says it hurts too much. She disappeared, a good few years before you did. They were very close. She was eleven years old.'

'Podge, I … I'm so sorry. I had no idea you had children. Was she ever found?'

'She was never found, no.' His eyes had gone red and wet. 'They told me she probably ran away, maybe to England, or something. I searched for many years. But I knew it wasn't England, or France or America she had gone to. People said I was mad, the way I went on about the old stories. How I searched for her there, in folklore, instead of out in the real world, whatever that is. But I know there is more to this land than modern people know. The old ways still thrive. It was the *Shee* that took her. I know it was.'

'The *Shee*?'

'Yes, the *Shee* are dark faeries. Goblins. Black as pitch. The same thing that tried to take you, Mary. The very same. When I found you, you tried to tell me about it. The creature.'

Mary couldn't find any words to reply.

They had arrived at the turn for Sheedys', and drove up to the farmhouse in silence. Mary parked up next to the unfinished building site, and took a torch from the

145

glovebox. The first thing they noticed was the scaffolding, collapsed in a heap. Under the pile was the crushed body of an expensive-looking jeep.

'What in God's name has happened here?' Mary asked.

Podge hushed her, putting a finger to his lips. It was very frightening, a place like this in half-darkness with only a small torch to see with.

'Quiet! There's someone here.'

'Oh, my God! You're scaring me now, Podge,' Sean's mother whispered.

The old man beckoned her to follow him, creeping around the back of the half-built outhouses. Around them the rain on the leaves sounded like a crowd in applause. Suddenly, Podge crouched and pulled Mary down beside him. He pointed down the garden. And before he could stop her, Mary pointed the torch beam in that direction.

Standing by a mound of grass and stone in the far corner was a priest. He was incredibly tall.

'Is that? It is! That's Fr Shanlon!' Mary hissed, 'The principal at St Augustin's! What's he doing out here?'

'Sssshhh! Turn that torch off!' Podge urged her. But it was too late. The tall priest turned in their direction. His eyes were like flashlights themselves. Mary couldn't believe what she was seeing. The man did not look real. Then she watched as he clicked his fingers, and her torch went dead.

The only thing to be seen in the dark were the two glowing, green globes of his eyes. They blinked once, twice and
then they too were gone. Mary banged her torch on her
palm, trying to get it going. It flickered back into life, but
Fr Shanlon was nowhere to be seen.

Moving cautiously among the strange, hazy pillars in Fal,
it was impossible for Benvy and Sean to see further than
a few metres ahead. The evening light was fading and the
patternless repetition of giant columns materialising from
the mist was totally disorientating. After half an hour they
were hopelessly lost – not that they were ever sure where
they were going to after they discovered that the city
turned out to be great stones.

'I really don't like this place,' Sean declared.

'What's to like, Sheridan? It's creepy as hell,' said Benvy.
She kept Ida close beside her.

As if on cue, a movement stopped all three in their
tracks. Just ahead, a faint shadow had darted between the
pillars, leaving the fog to coil lazily behind it. The little
group sprinted for cover and pressed their backs into a
cold column, trying to hide. There was a noise. It was distant, carried through the air in echoes among the stone.
It was hard to make out, but it was some kind of thud

followed by a ... snuffle? Whatever it was, it meant they weren't alone.

'I think we should run,' whispered Sean.

'Run where?' asked Benvy. 'There's nowhere to go!'

The noise came again, not closer but no less unsettling.

'Walk then! Let's just go somewhere!'

Carefully but quickly they moved forward, into the blinding white, away from where the shadow of whatever it was had appeared. At last, the scene changed: the ground dipped away into to a bowl and there were no more pillars. It was a relief to feel they were going somewhere, but unnerving to think they had left the protection of those strange obelisks. On the ground they could see a groove coiling from the centre of the bowl, in a spiral, out to its edges. After some tentative exploration, they realised they were still surrounded by the stone forest. They huddled near the bottom of the bowl, with their backs to each other and Ida between them. For a while, they could see nothing. Then, just metres away, the apparition reappeared, stopping and starting. As they watched it moved again, closer this time. Then, it stopped, turned and started to move directly towards them. Benvy got her javelin ready to throw, and elbowed Sean to get ready. He raised his hammer. When the ghostly figure finally appeared, and Benvy was just about to release her weapon, Sean surprised them all by laughing out loud.

'I don't believe it!' he said, lowering the hammer. 'Goll? Is that you?'

The figure was indeed a man; he was looking at Sean with an expression of utter bewilderment. He was young – maybe eighteen or nineteen, but Sean could still recognise him by his beak nose and tall, slender frame. It was definitely Goll, albeit a younger Goll than the one Sean had met before in Fal. Back when Ayla's uncle Fergus and Sean had found themselves prisoners at a Norman keep, it was this man who had helped them escape.

'Goll! It's me, Sean! From the Norman keep? With Fergus? And the whole … Oh, I've just realised. It hasn't happened to him yet.' Sean said this to Benvy, who was looking just as perplexed as the new arrival. 'You see,' muttered Sean, half to himself, 'this is where time-travel makes stuff confusing.'

'Eh, Sheridan, what is going on? Who is *Goll*? How do you know this guy? He doesn't seem to know you!' Benvy kept Ida behind her, and was still holding the javelin up defensively.

'Yeah, uh. Well, this is Goll. You remember the guy I told you all about, from Fal, who helped Fergus and myself escape when the Normans captured us? He had powers like Ayla.' Seeing Benvy's expression was still blank, Sean said lamely, 'But that was then, and, well, this is now.'

Losing her patience and not really understanding what

Sean was saying, Benvy snapped, 'What in God's name are you jabbering about?'

'Well, he doesn't know me, because what happened to us with the Normans hasn't happened yet. This is *young* Goll. And, uh, I just hope "young Goll" is as friendly as "old Goll".'

Young Goll, was very tall and thin. He was dressed in wool: a kind of belted dressing-gown with a big hood. He had no shoes and his head was shaved bald but for a long strand of dirty blond hair at the back which draped over one shoulder. He was looking at the group of friends with total confusion. Then he started to gesticulate wildly, and talk animatedly, becoming increasingly agitated with every word. He was pointing out into the mist, waving a hand. Then realising the others couldn't understand him, he reached inside his gown and produced a clump of herbs, a tangle of wiry stems with tiny leaves. He whispered something over them, and then shoved the entire lot into his mouth. He chewed loudly and, after some time, swallowed with difficulty. With that, his eyes rolled back in his head, and he uttered some unintelligible incantation, waving a hand in front of his lips and over his ears. Then he looked at Sean, Benvy and Ida.

'I am Goll,' he said, in broken English. But something was not quite right. Sean couldn't quite put his finger on what it was until suddenly it dawned on him: Goll's lips didn't match the words that came out of his mouth. It looked like he was being badly dubbed. 'Who are you please? How does the boy know my name?'

'Uh. This is so weird,' Benvy said.

'Wow,' said Sean. 'You can talk English! Sort of. Goll, it's me: Sean! Well, sorry, I know you don't know me yet. But you will. I think? This time thing is bloody confusing. Anyway, this is my friend Benvy. And this little girl is called Ida. We are trying to bring her home. I hope you can help!'

Goll seemed to ignore all this. 'You need to leave, now, in hurry,' he said urgently. 'Not alone here.'

As soon as he said it, the strange noise they heard before Goll appeared came again from the fog. *Thump! Thump!* This time, it was close.

'Oh crap,' Goll said, in a badly lip-synced way, which unnerved the friends even more. 'Now we all leave!'

But they were too late. The source of the pounding appeared: an enormous muscular bull the size of a truck with long, gold-tipped horns that swooped out before it. On top of the bull was a man. Or at least, some kind of man. His eyes were effervescent red and two deer-like antlers protruded from his forehead. Sean remembered the stone sentinel statue. It was as if he has come to life. The giant rider carried a thick pole of red-gold that ended in a chunky chain. At the end of that was a curved blade like a crescent moon. He bellowed something in a voice that sounded like the noise of a crowd. Steam rushed out in blasts from the bull's wide nostrils and it stamped a huge hoof.

'RUN!' shouted Goll just before the beast charged.

The ground shook as if hammered by the fists of a god. The bull and rider roared furiously together, both sets of eyes wide and burning fiercely. The warrior rider's blade sang a shrill note as it sliced the mist. Benvy moved to carry Ida, but found Goll had already lifted the little girl in his arms. They all half-fell, half-ran, hauling each other along in a desperate attempt to escape. They ran with heaving lungs and burning throats, on into the grey fog and into the rows of columns. Behind them the shaking ceased; there was a snort and then there was silence.

Sean was the first to stop, unable to continue.

'W … Wait! Please! Stop! I have to stop!' He had his hands on his knees and the hammer at his feet. 'I can't run with this thing!'

'Is it gone? Are they gone? I can't see anything!' Benvy asked, also out of breath.

Goll replied: 'Not gone. Hunting. We must move.' He took up Sean's hammer, shifting Ida to his other hip and urged Sean to continue.

'Goll,' Sean gasped. 'Can't you do your magic? Bring a storm?'

'Magic? I no like. Me, poet.'

'But … you just *did* some. You're doing some now! Speaking English!'

'Ah … Yes. I dabble. But storms? That is for the Old Ones.'

They set off again, following Goll – who at least seemed to know where he was going.

'What was that thing? That bull is bigger than any I've seen before,' said Benvy.

'Magic folk. A guard, of these stones. Danann. They don't like us much. People, I mean.'

'So we're not meant to be here? What were *you* doing here then?'

'Me? Dabbling.'

On they went among the giant trunks of stone, turning every now and again with great caution, for fear the bull rider might return. There was still no sound.

'Agh,' Goll said eventually, halting the group. 'Not good.'

'What's not good?' Benvy asked.

'Lost.'

He suddenly jolted a hand up to silence them. He listened. They turned to a wide avenue they could see between the columns. The mist was rolling gently through the columns in thick curls.

'Why is the mist moving like that?' Sean asked.

The bull burst through the veil in a cacophony of black fury, bounding towards them with horns low enough to plough great furrows into the ground before it. The rider swung his weapon in howling arcs above his head. In the same split second, Benvy threw her javelin with all her might, but it did not scream or light up as it always had done. It landed harmlessly in the path of the great bull and was flung aside in a great wave of earth. There was no time left. The hunter was upon them.

With a great *KABOOOM!* the bull suddenly found itself swatted to one side, crashing into a pillar which wavered with the impact. Clumps of earth rained down from the blast, while the bull and the rider lay motionless. The group stood frozen in shock. Sean, Benvy and Ida stared at Goll.

Finally, Sean found his voice. 'Not into magic eh?' he asked, wide-eyed.

'Not me,' Goll replied, pointing over their shoulders. 'Him.'

The others spun on their heels and saw a tall, bald priest approaching them through the swirling dust.

The Citadel in the Cliffs

While Sean and Benvy made for the misty pillars, Ayla and Finny were following the young warrior, Lorcan, towards the coast. Lorcan was lithe and moved quickly across the landscape. Often he slowed to allow Ayla to keep up and they talked for long periods in their ancient Gaelic tongue. Finny followed behind, still nursing bruises inside and out. He refused to give in to jealousy, but when the pair laughed together it burned in him fiercely.

For Ayla's part, she found the strange young warrior a

baffling mix of unlikeable dork and fascinatingly exotic. Lorcan spoke in equal measure of his love for the land, the sea and his people, but just when he seemed the tiniest bit humble he would ruin it by reverting to cockiness. He boasted often of his prowess in battle, and rarely passed over an opportunity to show her just how dextrous he was. Lorcan back-flipped over boulders, or flung a stone from his sling only to sprint and catch it. Finny could barely disguise his disgust. Humility was not the warrior's strong point, Ayla figured, but it was obvious his intelligence matched his body in agility. He spoke of the things he loved with a poetic lilt, and the old language leant itself well to such idyllic descriptions. Of course, she struggled to comprehend how she was suddenly able to speak in a whole new tongue. But then, so much of what she was now was beyond her control. *I'm on auto-pilot, or worse,* she thought, maybe *someone else has the controls.*

Lorcan, she learned, was indeed a warrior, born to fight and trained to do so from the moment he could hold his own head up. He had just earned his marks – the freshly cut spirals that scoured his flesh – and he considered himself already one of the greatest fighters in Fal. That he had a high opinion of himself was an understatement. He didn't walk; he swaggered and strutted. But Ayla surprised herself by finding him enjoyable company, and it was a relief to finally laugh after so much wreckage. There was even a tiny part of her that almost enjoyed Finny's obvious jealousy.

'So where are you taking us?' she asked him, revelling in the fluency of her new tongue.

'I am taking you to a king who will help you, Storm Weaver.'

'Storm Weaver? Why do you call me that? Where did you get that name from?'

'That is what you are, isn't it? You can weave the wind and thunder. You can make lightning land on a single grain of sand. You can grip a hurricane and bend it to your will. I have heard tales about you since I can remember. You were the story that was meant to scare us into being good! You were the story that kept us awake at night.'

'But I don't understand. All I know is: I have to find Maeve. I have to find her ...'

Ayla paused. She wanted to say 'and kill her', but the words wouldn't come out. Her mind swam and she felt dizzy.

'It is ... complicated.' Lorcan said, looking her in the eye. 'The game of war starts long before the battlefield. I am young but I have been playing for a long time. There will be a battle, and it is my job to get you to the right side. But to do that, I have had to play on both.'

Finny had caught up.

'Sorry to interrupt,' he said. 'But that huge bird has been

circling us for the last few miles. Are we prey? I don't want to be eaten.'

At that moment, a piercing scream echoed amongst the rocks from high in the air. It was indeed a huge bird: a hawk or something like it. It swept across the sky in great arcs, and cast a large shadow when it passed in front of the sun. Lorcan's face took on a strange expression. It was almost fearful at first; then it darkened to a scowl.

'Well? Is it going to eat us?' Finny asked again.

'Our course has changed' was Lorcan's only answer. 'And so, Storm Weaver, has the game.'

They had been following the line of the forest around to the left, leaving the mountain behind and keeping the distant ocean to their right. Lorcan changed direction, turning towards the coast. Finny and Ayla shrugged at each other and joined him. They could see that the confident Lorcan was now troubled, and he did not speak again for a long time, though he looked up to the bird often.

Now the way ahead was mostly barren: sheets of bare rock, scored with deep fissures, lay in plates piled awkwardly together so that sudden inland cliff-like obstacles were common, and the only easy way to the coast was with one who knew the way. Lorcan reckoned on at least two days' travel to their final destination by foot if they 'weren't slowed down' – a slight aimed squarely at Finny, with little subtlety. They slept that night by a river that carved the limestone in a deep fissure across the landscape. They woke before sunrise to resume their journey. The hawk still circled: the last thing they saw at night, and the first upon waking.

It had taken them until mid-afternoon to reach land's end, where the air was briny and sweet. Great sea-arches extended into the waves from the cliffs like buttresses, and the sea rolled slowly through them to detonate against the bluffs. Gulls sailed the thermals, their calls lost in the relentless thunder of the tide. The weather was fine, but cold, with cotton-ball clouds, fat with rain, herded slowly inland by invisible fronts. The whole scene served to lift the spirits. Ayla turned to Finny and smiled. He smiled back, but his smile soon dropped from his face when Lorcan brushed passed his shoulder, carrying a heavy skin of water. Ayla had been smiling at the young warrior, not Finny.

They stopped for a break, and Lorcan left them to drink and rest while he went off in search of food. It was the last fresh water they would see until the end of their journey, so they had to be conservative. Finny swished a mouthful and spat.

'Finny! Don't waste it! Lorcan said …'

'"*Lorcan said* "yadda yadda"!' Even Finny recognised the childishness in his own voice, but he couldn't help himself. 'And whatever Lorcan says is true, right?'

'Finny, don't be a doofus,' Ayla said flatly. 'He's helping us. Where would we be without him?'

'*We* would be nowhere. *You* would be on your own if I hadn't followed you. And this entire time you haven't mentioned Sean or Benvy once! I mean, come on, Ayla, we have just left our two best friends in the world, you know? In a place that is, well, a little far from home, to say the least! And you've been laughing and talking with that fool as if this was some sort of holiday!'

Anger was really bubbling up inside him now. He knew from past experience that it was too late to stop it.

'Finny, that's not …'

'What? Fair? I wonder if Sean and Benvy think it's fair? Or that little girl, if she really is all innocent like Benvy says? Or Lann, Fergus and Taig for that matter! Did they die so that you could abandon your friends?'

He regretted the words even as he said them. But his blood was hot and the flush of temper deadened the guilt.

Ayla didn't speak. She stood up and walked away and Finny was left alone to ruminate. After a while, a wet Lorcan returned laden with shellfish; he had even caught two lobsters and a few small crabs. He dropped them at Finny's feet and laughed when the boy wrenched his legs away, afraid of the claws. It was the first time Lorcan has smiled since the hawk had appeared. He brought some driftwood too, and made short work of lighting a fire with a flint. When it was underway, he turned to watch the distant speck of Ayla looking out over the ocean. He jabbed a thumb in her direction and said something.

Finny was still angry. 'I … don't … understand … you,' he said, frowning.

Lorcan nodded to Ayla again, and then pointed a finger at Finny and said a word that had survived the ages in the Irish language.

'*Amadán.*' Idiot.

Too right, thought Finny, but not out loud.

As Ayla and Finny encountered the huge bird in the sky and changed their direction to make their way across the stony plains to the ocean, Sean, Benvy and Ida were trying to make sense of their situation and the sudden arrival of a priest with some sort of magical powers.

'We won't dally,' the lanky priest said to the stunned group. 'It is nearly night and that Danann guard will be awake again soon.'

As if to drive home the point, the giant beast jerked and slowly started to breathe again.

'You … You're a priest! Like, an Irish one. From home!' Sean exclaimed.

The priest made an expression as if to say 'sometimes'.

'Yes I am … often … a priest. You might know me as Fr Shanlon, from St Augustin's School. But here in Fal, I am known as Cathbad and I am a druid.'

Sean looked puzzled; something about the name *Cathbad* seemed to ignite some distant memory in him. Benvy, however, was nodding.

'You're *the* Fr Shanlon, right? As in: The Streak! Taig told me about you. He said you were really a … what was it?' Benvy asked.

His deep-set green eyes flashed as he peered down over his thick glasses. Benvy seemed to shrink a couple of centimetres.

'Cathbad will do, child.'

Goll was kneeling with head bowed. He spoke in his native tongue, and this time his lips moved in sync with the strange words.

'The honour is mine, Goll,' Cathbad replied. 'You may get up now. No time for formalities.'

A deep groan came from behind the prone bull.

'Quickly, now.'

They had to run after Cathbad's long gait through the fog and out from among the pillars. It took half an hour before they were out in the open again, and in a strange transition the mist broke only feet from the last column. Here, the night was crisp and the air was moist and sweet. The sun had disappeared; a crescent moon had replaced it, and a swathe of stars glinted in the navy sky.

'We will walk a little, and then you may sleep. We cannot journey in darkness, but we will leave just before sunrise.'

'What about the bull? Shouldn't we be running?' Benvy asked, shivering against the cold.

'He is not able to leave the Pillars. You are safe from him at least.'

The druid turned to Goll, and said something to him in his native tongue.

Goll looked sheepish.

Cathbad proceeded to explain the situation to the others, 'Goll here will remain safe as long as he doesn't go snooping around where he shouldn't be again. The Pillars of the Danann are no place for a young man to go in search of magic. Also, he is going to travel with us. We're all going in the same direction, after all.'

Sean had been muttering to himself, desperately trying to coax the memory of where he'd heard Cathbad's name from the back of his brain.

'But hang on,' he held a hand up, like he was in a classroom. 'I know you from somewhere! Who are you exactly?'

Cathbad was enormously tall. He had a large beak nose that arched out over a thin-lipped mouth, seemingly set in permanent grimace. His eyes, set in deep recesses behind thick glasses, were mesmerising, twinkling like emeralds.

'As I said, child, I am Cathbad. I am a druid, and one of

a council that folk like Goll call "The Old Ones". In fact, some might say, I am *the* Old One. The others are a little younger.'

'Uh huh,' Benvy confirmed, as if she knew everything.

Sean suddenly snapped his fingers, remembering. When Fergus had told him the story of Queen Maeve, he had mentioned a Cathbad – the druid that fought Maeve and her lover and rescued Ayla as a baby.

Benvy was delighted that she was more clued up than Sean was, for once.

'But, back where you come from, your friend Oscar Finnegan knows me as Fr Shanlon. I am his principal in St Augustin's. Troublesome boy, that one.'

He'd cause a lot less trouble if he knew who you really were, Sean thought, *and what you could do.*

A long-fingered hand was raised to silence any further questions. 'All in good time.'

Not knowing quite why, Sean and Benvy made a decision to trust this 'priest'. After all, he had just saved their lives. They realised that they had no real choice but to follow him.

Cathbad led them down a gentle decline, and then said they would rest by a tall boulder. Goll made a fire and, with the heat beginning to rise from the flames, he curled up into his robes and, before long, was snoring loudly. The others huddled together on the other side of the fire and did their best to protect each other from the cold. Cathbad perched himself on top of the rock and told them to sleep, and that he would keep watch. It took a long time to drift off, and morning came all too soon.

In the first grey light the land spread out in a flat expanse to the horizon. As the sun climbed, the colour returned with the green grass of the mountains seeping into a vast plain of mustard bogland. On the marsh, light from the new sun showed numerous bodies of water: puddles, ponds and lakes scattered across the plain like silver coins. In the distance, barely visible, a bank of hills stood like a giant wave.

'You'll want to take your shoes off and roll up your britches,' Cathbad instructed. 'The going from here will be muddy and wet. On the way, we will talk,' he said, pre-empting the next battery of questions that teetered on Sean and Benvy's lips.

'Have you food? If so, eat it on the go. We are in a hurry; time is our enemy now.'

Cathbad set off down the slope. He was deceptively quick for an old man, and their curiosity would have to wait.

By midday, they were squelching ankle-deep in soft mud. It was a struggle, with every footstep a tiring tug from the sucking clay. They avoided the pools, follow-ing the course set by Cathbad (who seemed to meet no resistance in the mire) among the stiff ochre grasses. Occasionally, they would find a solid path between the tufts and were grateful for the break, but the pace was rigorous and, more often than not, they had to run on those firmer trails. Goll carried Ida on his shoulders for much of the time, and he sang to her as they went. The melody cheered Sean and Benvy, and for the first time in an age, they felt a modicum of hope. After hours of silence, the priest spoke at last.

'Well, you have questions, I presume?'

Sean and Benvy looked at each other. Benvy ventured to speak first, but Fr Shanlon cut her off.

'First, I have some. Who is this young one?'

'This is Ida, Father,' Sean replied, addressing Cathbad as a priest.

Cathbad frowned for a moment, as if he was unsure of something, and was searching his memory for the answer. Then he seemed to shrug it off.

'No need for "Father" here, lad. You may recognise me as a priest, but here, as I said, my name is Cathbad. And where did this Ida come from?'

'Cathbad. Sorry. Ida is a girl we rescued from the caves, from that mad queen, Maeve. When we went to find Ayla. Ida was one of those creatures that helped kidnap Ayla.

Cathbad stopped for a moment. He looked at Ida, contemplating something but again shrugged it off. It was almost like he thought he knew her.

'A girl, you say? Down in the caves. And she has not told you where she is from?'

'She can't talk! The only thing she has been able to say is her name.'

Sean and Benvy recounted the whole story as they walked.

Benvy couldn't help but say what she thought of how their friend Ayla had been acting, and how Finny sided with her and was suspicious of Ida: '… And so we had a fight. Ayla was acting all weird, and Finny didn't trust Ida. That big idiot thought she might be dangerous! Imagine that? I mean, you know him, right? Big, tough Oscar Finnegan: hard-lad and bona-fide bad boy. Frightened of a girl! And, well …' Benvy tried to remain defiant, but choked on the next few words, 'Ayla and Finny left us. But we don't need them. We're going to get Ida home without them.'

For a long time Cathbad said nothing.

'I'm afraid, child, that may not be possible. It may not be possible for any of you to return.'

Benvy and Sean stopped.

'What? Why? We thought you were going to help!' Benvy's voice was raised now and she started to shake slightly.

'Where are we going, Cathbad? We want to know right

now!' Sean was also shouting.

'We are going to Tara, lad. To meet with Brú, the High King of Men. Then, we are going to war.'

The further along the coast they went, the deeper Ayla's silence bore into Finny. They were travelling north along jutting headlands and across coarse, tawny beaches. The wheeling speck of the hawk never left the sky above them, and Lorcan still looked up to it often, nervously. There were no trees and little grass, and the gashes in the rock were often deep and wide and made for hair-raising jumps. Finny refused to show any fear, but he couldn't rely on help from Lorcan or from Ayla. She was completely withdrawn from him. And she didn't seem to need Lorcan's help. She never looked back to see how her friend fared, not even when one of his jumps fell short and left him scrabbling to reach the other side of a deep gash in the rocks. They had travelled a full day in this way, and slept the night among undulating dunes. The next morning they were off again and now it was late afternoon. The sun was high but there was little warmth, and a legion of clouds was approaching from the sea, heralded by a quickening wind.

The flats had given way to hills, and they had traversed

three high promontories, descending the third as the rain made land. From here the terrain oscillated in ever-greater surges until the hills became mountains that held one foot in the ocean. They walked through the last vale, facing the range and, dreading the climb, Lorcan stopped and spoke to Ayla. Finny hung back.

They took a few minutes' rest in the shelter of the first tree they had seen in days – a crooked hawthorn, deadened by the salty air. Lorcan slapped Finny on the arm, nodding to a gully in the foothills ahead. It was a couple of metres wide, and cut straight through the escarpment like a knife wound.

'So that's where we're going?' Finny pointed, to be clear.

Lorcan nodded, and where once he had sported an infuriating grin, his jaw was clenched and his brow furrowed. As he moved away, Finny returned to fantasies of beating the warrior to a pulp.

When the rain eased off, they gathered themselves and headed for the gully. It was close to the oceanward side of the hill that ended with the slope cleaved into a cliff. The sea threw itself against it in vengeful heaves.

In the pass through the mountain, it was gloomy and cold. The path went downwards so that the walls of rock stretched up forever on either side until the sky became nothing more than a slit of white. It was slippy and at places too tight to walk head-on. Those squeezes brought up bleak memories of the tunnels and heaped more unhappiness on a very low Finny. He really wasn't sure if he had made the right choice in leaving his friends behind. It seemed to him that Ayla was beyond help.

I hope they are okay. I hope Benvy wants to make up. I hope we see each other again.

The gully pass remained straight for a long time, and then gently began to curve to the right. At last, the walls lowered, the claustrophobia eased and they emerged into a bay that could only be described as a dream.

The cove was a kilometre across and surrounded by a cliff eight hundred metres tall. The sea rolled onto a beach of smooth, round stones that chattered every time the water receded, loud enough to hear even from where they stood. The arm of land on the opposite side was hollowed out by caves of incredible size. Where they met the sea, the caves became arches, and the arches became stacks – a dozen of them in a line. On each there was a statue, just like the stone sentinel by the lake, but erect, looking out to sea. The sea caves did not all look entirely natural. On some the curvature was too perfect to be made by the sea, and on others there were decorative carvings on a breathtaking scale. Behind the beach was a city.

Buildings that looked grown rather than built clustered around an imposing, balconied citadel. The stone was twisted and moulded into halls, temples and houses.

The buildings were organic, flowing and sinuous. The citadel itself was hewn from the cliff, all wide platforms and colonnades of sandstone and shale. It looked like a many-limbed creature climbing onto the bluff.

Finny and Ayla stood and stared for a long time, unable to speak. Then once again the air was split with the cry of the hawk. They felt the air behind them beaten and heard the sound of great wings. They ducked, and Finny thought they were about to be carried away by some great talons, but Lorcan was staring over their shoulders, and then he bowed and dropped to one knee. They turned.

A woman was standing in the passage from where they had just come from. She was immensely tall – Sean guessed about two-and-a-half metres at least – and was clothed in flowing green silk with a wide hood draped over her head. The shoulders of the cloak were coated in brown feathers. Her long face was graceful and pale, with high oval cheek-bones framed with pitch-black hair that fell out over the robes, billowing in the wind. In the shadow of the cowl her eyes glowed like lava. When she spoke, her voice mirrored the clattering stones in the wash on the beach. Finny didn't understand, but Ayla spoke to him for the first time in ages, albeit without eye contact.

'She says we have to go with her. We are to meet with her king, and then her god.'

The Red Horizon

To Sean and Benvy the way through the marshes had seemed eternal, and weariness trampled over them pitilessly. They had run out of toad meat ages ago, but while Goll had a knack for catching food in unlikely places (the taste of fat bog slugs would never leave them), it was not enough to sustain three children. Cathbad never seemed interested in food and had little patience for slow walkers, and so the pace rarely slackened; the breaks were always too short and the journey had taken a heavy toll.

Cathbad did, however, make time to explain his presence in Fal. He told them the story of how men had lived in Fal long before the arrival of a magical race known as the Danann (the bullrider in the pillars had been one of them). A high council of druids was elected; Cathbad was the leader, and he was to act as a go-between between the two races: humans and the Danann. The Danann shared some secrets of their magic with the council while, in turn, the people of Fal allowed them land in the west, to settle. They had lived in relative harmony for many years until one of the council, a druid-queen from the south called Maeve, fell in love with a dark Danann sorcerer. Her thirst for more magical power grew ever more intense. She declared herself a queen and with the sorcerer sought outright control of Fal. The druids banished Maeve and the Red Root King; that much Sean and Benvy knew already, and Ayla was their child. But after the banishment, the trust between the two sides was lost, and relations between the Danann and the people of Fal were forever soured.

'Our first fear was that, if Ayla should ever be captured by Maeve, the evil queen would return to her full strength and attempt to regain control of Fal. If that happened, the future of ordinary people would be destroyed. You children would not exist. Ireland would not exist. There would be only darkness.

'But now, it seems, this is not the full picture. Ayla

returned to Fal: something that should never have happened. She is being *drawn* here by something. There is war brewing between man and Danann and we, the Council, fear Ayla has a part to play in this that could swing the outcome in their favour. The Danann are plotting something, and Maeve is somehow involved. And so I have returned. That you happened to be in the Pillars when I returned was pure coincidence.'

Cathbad did not seem to welcome a discussion after his explanation. He had told them what they needed to know, and then, he declared, it was time for him to think on matters while they walked. And so Sean and Benvy were left to talk among themselves and try to comprehend the situation. They had seen enough over the last while not to be surprised by the existence of a magical race intent on war. But the thought of their friend Ayla having a large role to play in it troubled them. Ayla was in danger, and the way Cathbad had said she was 'being *drawn* here' – that meant she was not entirely in control of herself. That explained a lot to Benvy, and she felt bad that she had been so angry with Ayla.

Both of them were by now very tired, but Sean found it in himself to urge Benvy on and ignore his own suffering. His time in the tunnels, alone in the dark always a hair's breath from death, had given the boy a steely inner strength. He had to draw deeply from it now. When Benvy stumbled, Sean helped her up. He carried her javelin and tried to tell jokes that really he knew just annoyed her, but at least they were a distraction. He did his time carrying Ida on his back too, when she needed it, to give Goll a rest.

Goll had taken more of the strange grass that made him talk like he was in an old kung-fu movie, and he explained to Sean a little of how it worked. He spoke of how magic and botany went hand in hand, but too much of either was bad.

In return, Sean did his best to explain their backstory. 'You see, me and Benvy are from Fal too. But it's Fal thousands of years in the future, and it's called "Ireland".'

Goll curled his lip in confusion.

'Ayla is our best friend. And she got kidnapped by goblins and brought to some underground hellhole. And Lann, Fergus and Taig – the 'Sons of Cormac' as you called them – they were her uncles. Well, not really. But anyway, they were able to bring us back though burial mounds to ancient times so we could rescue Ayla. Well, ancient times to us. And me and Fergus got a bit lost and ended up in a different time than we had intended: in Norman times. Where we met you, Goll. In your future. Oh, my God, this is impossible.' Sean gave up.

'It sound like work of Old Ones to me. Druids, like him,' Goll nodded at Cathbad. 'He is the oldest, and the most powerful.'

'If he is so powerful,' asked Sean, 'why can't he and his council just kill Maeve once and for all, rescue Ayla and send us home?'

'I do not understand the ways of the Old Ones. But remember: the Old Ones got their magic from the Danann. The Danann are more powerful. Too much magic, I think. For me, I only like to dabble. Tricks. I will show you some.'

'Well, you say you only like to dabble. But what were you doing in those pillars? And, by the way, when I met you before? You knew a lot more than tricks. You could control the weather!'

Goll stopped and stared at the boy.

'Me? A Storm Weaver? I don't think so, boy. Yes, okay. I would like to maybe learn some more magic, but storm-leashing is for the druids. My young brother, he is the warrior. And I am not so good with a sword, but with tricks? I am good. Also, with my sling.'

To prove this, Goll spun the sling expertly round his head but then for a time was silent. The thought that he might gain 'Storm Weaver' status, whatever that was, seemed to trouble him. After a while, Sean urged him back into conversation and got him to teach him a couple of his tricks. Like how to clap loud enough that the ribs of those around you rattled with the vibration (it didn't go down well with the others) and how to throw a rock so that it flew like a bullet and exploded like a banger (again, unpopular with the rest of the group). It really came down to a few simple incantations, the right sleight-of-hand, and a lot of practice. Goll said that Sean was a natural, which pleased him no end. He wanted Benvy to see his new tricks, but she looked too tired to notice anything.

Speaking with Goll and learning tricks helped Sean cope with the hard travelling. Ida seemed to find energy from things in the grass that excited her. She had pulled up a tuft of stiff yellow grass and stuffed it into her pocket, and on another occasion seemed particularly happy to find a small clutch of delicate, purple flowers growing from the stagnant water of a bog pool. It was nice to see her with a smile on her face.

Benvy was really not faring so well.

While Ida scoured the marsh for herbs and flowers, Sean and Goll were giggling and performing tricks, Benvy was left alone to drift away in thought. She struggled, for the most part, to keep them positive. She missed home terribly, and thought about how her brother and parents were probably beside themselves with worry. She tried as hard as she could to estimate how long they had been away, but it was impossible. So much had happened that time had lost all relevance. It was only about going forward, never stopping, even when the entire universe seemed determined to crash down around them in shards. But just as soon as Benvy reached her lowest ebb and thought about just sitting there and giving up, Sean would appear beside her and make some stupid joke designed specifically to annoy her (on purpose she knew). Or Goll would take a pensive Ida back in his arms and strike up a playful melody again. Benvy hadn't even really properly registered that they'd left the bog and were now walking through tall green grass.

Evening was falling on yet another day in Fal, and this time the sky was gashed with a deeper blood-red sunset than they had ever seen before. Cathbad watched the horizon with a troubled look on his face. They made a simple camp in a field flanked by hills, where massive oaks and sycamores hulked, dwarfing the trees in Coleman's.

'I've never seen a sky like that, have you, Benv'?' Sean asked.

'No! It's like someone has cut the sky, and it's pumping blood.'

Cathbad called for their attention.

'Tonight, you may rest well. We are another day from our destination, but the rest of the trip will be made in good company.'

He left the last few words unexplained, and Goll was instructed to build a big fire. Sean and Ida went with him to help get firewood while Benvy and Cathbad were left alone.

'I could have helped too, Fath … Cathbad.'

'Better you rest, child. You seem in need of it.'

'Yeah, I'm pretty bushed.' Benvy sat without need of further invitation.

'Cathbad?'

'Yes.'

'What do you talk about? To Ida, I mean? I'd love to able to speak to her.'

'You will, child. In time, she will speak. As for what I talk about, a great many things, young Benvy. I am trying to coax the words from her, and to make sure she is not going to give us any trouble. We do not know what so long under the mask of a goblin has done to her.'

'That's what Finny thought! But look at her: she's just frightened!'

'Yes, I know. But I have to be sure. I have an idea I may know who this girl is. A girl from Kilnabracka, no less.'

'What? From *our* Kilnabracka? How …?'

'I think fate may have had a hand in finding her among the others, Benvy. She spoke of you very highly. You saved her more than once, it seems.'

'Yeah. Well, she's just a little girl, isn't she?'

'If she is who I think she might be, she should be, oh …' he paused to calculate, '… about fifty-eight, I think.'

Benvy was shocked.

'But where she has been, she has not aged. Her time in the clutches of the Red Root King took its toll. As it did on *you*.' Cathbad looked her in the eye now. 'As it did on all of you. You have done many great things, Benvy Caddock. I think you should know that.'

It felt strange, receiving a compliment from this druid. He did not seem like a man who would give out many, so it was appreciated.

'Of course, you all did a very stupid thing when you went back down into those tunnels. That should never have happened. You played directly into our enemy's hands.'

'I had my doubts,' said Benvy. 'I mean, I didn't want us to risk our lives again when we had only just escaped with them. But surely it was the right thing to do, to try and rescue those girls?'

'Right in terms of morals? Yes. It was brave and selfless. And Ida thanks you for it. But tell me, how long did it take before you realised the real reason for Ayla's return?'

Benvy didn't need to think about it.

'Not long! It might have been the reason to get us back initially, but then Ayla seemed to forget about saving the girls pretty quickly! She was just obsessed with finding Maeve. Everything else stopped mattering. Even her friends.'

'It wasn't her fault, young Benvy. She could not have helped that.'

'But what about all that magic? All the power she has?

She's some kind of sorceress now, right?'

'Child,' he looked her dead in the eye again, 'how do you think she came by that power?'

'Her uncles, Lann and Fergus MacCormac.' She still couldn't bring herself to mention Taig. 'They gave it to her. When they saved her, right?'

For a second the image of the giant brothers' bodies crumbling and taking off on the wind like ash, filled Benvy's mind. The memory of the three uncles giving their lives for Ayla would never leave her.

'No, child, they did not give her anything but her life back. Did the power grow the deeper into the tunnels you went? Think.'

'Yes, it did!'

'The power comes from *Maeve*. This unquenchable thirst for the hunt: also from Maeve. She is the Lost Sister of the Old Ones, and she has called her daughter to her, and with every step closer, the magic consumes Ayla more. I fear, by now, she may be lost.'

Of course! That was what he meant by Ayla being 'drawn' here. It made sense to Benvy now, how Ayla had acted so selfishly. She was under some kind of spell. She was turning into something else.

'The Lost Sister? What does that mean?'

'Maeve was once of my order, an Earth-Sister, one of the Old Ones. We were here in Fal before the Danann.

There were many struggles when the Danann came. We tried to live together but they wanted to rule over Fal. The power we traded with the Danann was not enough. And, as I said, Maeve began to crave power of her own ...'

Here his voice faltered, just for a second.

'But I think that is enough for now. Time for you to eat, I see.'

Three dead rabbits landed on the ground beside her.

'I caught those! And get this: I did it by *whistling*!' Sean stood, grinning at Benvy. 'Goll showed me! How cool is that?'

Benvy just stared at Sean and Goll without speaking.

'What?' said Sean, and got no reply.

Cathbad headed off into the lengthening shadows.

While Sean and Benvy were crossing the great marsh, Finny and Ayla had made their way into the halls of the citadel by the ocean. Finny felt like he had been swallowed by a whale. The halls of the citadel could not have been carved by hand unless there had been hundreds or thousands of years to do it. They looked more like they'd been eaten away by some monstrous worm and then decorated in obsessive detail.

Lorcan had not come with them into the citadel itself

and instead had gone off into the busy streets. He seemed to feel quite at home here, even if he looked nothing like the city's inhabitants. All of the people were like the woman who had brought them down from the pass: tall, strong and regal. The men looked oddest of all, massive and tall with long forked antlers, while man, woman and child all had the same unsettling red glow in their eyes. The streets of the city itself were bustling, with the throng of strange folk all busy with something: lifting, packing, hauling. But inside the citadel the halls were laden with a sacred silence and were mostly empty, except for the green-cloaked guards that stood among the pillars.

Ayla evidently no longer felt any responsibility to translate for Finny or to communicate with him in any way. He tried numerous times to snap her out of it, offering apologies and reasoning that he had been punished enough. But Ayla was cold and unresponsive, following the tall woman unquestioningly and ignoring Finny's pleas for peace. *She's like a zombie*, he thought, and he felt very, very alone.

They were led in silence to a huge round hall. In the centre of the hall was a white pile of marble that looked as though it had been melted, poured and set again, if such a thing were possible. On top of this was a throne, slender and simple, made of bone-coloured wood and left to its natural shape. On the throne was a king.

He was just as tall as the rest of the citadel's people, and no older than any of the men Finny had seen (in fact, they had all seemed rather young-looking now that he thought about it). But there were two major differences, as far as Finny could see. Firstly, the king's antlers were not those of a deer. Finny had seen something like them before, on some school trip to the Natural History Museum. They were the huge, wide antlers of an elk. Secondly, unlike all of the other 'men', the king had a long beard of straight red hair. It jarred a little with his youthfulness, but certainly set him apart from the rest of his people.

He beckoned an aide to come to him with a bowl of something green, which he ate quickly and silently. Then he whispered something to himself, waved a hand in front of his mouth and around his ears, and began to speak. To Finny's great surprise – the king spoke in English.

'Ah. Thank the God, Lorcan has brought you here safely. He is a good lad. Welcome to the home of my people, The Danann. I am Nuada.'

The king shifted on his chair.

'I did not expect you to arrive with company, I must admit. This one must be stubborn.'

He nodded in the direction of Finny. Ayla said nothing. *It's like she's asleep,* Finny thought. He also noticed that there was something strange about the way the king was talking. King Nuada's lips were not quite matching his words. They seemed out of time, like a badly dubbed film.

'In any case, it is a joyous thing that you are here. And at last, we can help you. Ayla, daughter of Maeve, you will achieve your destiny!'

Ayla broke her silence at last: 'Maeve? You will help me to find her?'

The king smiled. 'Yes, child. We will help you to end your search. And then you will help us, I hope, in what is to come.'

To this, Ayla made no reply.

'We do not have a lot of time. I will take you to see the Dagda.'

'The Dagda?' Ayla asked.

'Our God. He wishes to speak with you.'

Ayla did not seem surprised by this talk of a god and she simply nodded as if this was not a strange thing to be told.

'Boy,' the king turned to address Finny.

'Eh, yeah … Yes … Your Highness?'

Finny was never good at communicating with figures of authority. He could see irritation flitting across Nuada's face.

Gesturing towards the woman who had brought Finny and Ayla into the citadel, the king said, 'You cannot go where the girl goes. You will be looked after by Nemain here.'

'But …'

Finny's protest was cut short as Nemain took him gently

but firmly by the arm and led him out of the hall. Ayla never even looked back at her friend once.

There was no breaking Nemain's grip. It was not so tight as to be uncomfortable, but Finny could not shake it, and no matter how much he protested, her hand didn't move even one inch. Nemain escorted him into the thrumming streets of the city, and she did it in silence. Up ahead, a crowd had gathered in a square and were cheering at some unseen spectacle. Finny was released and, without a word, Nemain turned her back, raised her arms and in a second transformed into a hawk. She flew back to the citadel as Finny looked on, amazed at her metamorphosis.

A regular crowd that bayed like that could be unnerving. But being three metres tall with antlers and glowing red eyes, it was positively frightening. Still Finny edged forward towards the cheering crowd, his curiosity giving him courage. One advantage to being half their size was he found it quite easy to squeeze past them to the front. Finny spotted Lorcan and one of the horned men in the centre of the crowd locked in some sort of contest. It was some kind of combat combined with sport. They each held a wooden, paddle-shaped weapon, a little like a hurl – if a hurl was modified more effectively for killing. It was planed to a sharp edge on one side, on the part that curved backwards. They were contesting a black ball that seemed to be made of something heavy and polished, like black onyx. Each stood in front of a panel of wood with a single hole cut out. The goal, Finny guessed. They lunged for the ball.

Lorcan was tiny compared to his opponent, but he was lightning-quick and clearly revelled in the scrap. That infuriating grin never left his face, even when he was struck. From sport Finny knew that extreme confidence was an advantage on the playing field, and Lorcan had more than enough of that. For one brief moment, it seemed as though the great antlered man would win, hitting Lorcan with an unmerciful backhand on the side of his face and scooping up the ball. He was inches from placing it in the hole when Lorcan sprang up and clambered on to this opponent, wrapping his arms and legs around him like a boa, just as he had with Finny when they first met. The deer-man fought to put the onyx sphere through the board and was agonisingly close, but his face had turned puce and was all puffed up from the exertion. Then his burning eyes dimmed as they rolled back, and, with an almighty thump, he fell, unconscious.

Lorcan picked up the ball and, over-dramatically, on one tippy-toe, placed the ball in his opponent's goal. He raised his arms in triumph, though there were few cheers. Lorcan didn't seem to be enjoying this victory as much as Finny thought he would. The grin seemed just for show, as his eyes were constantly darting to the citadel and the sea-caves. The young warrior seemed anxious, as if he wanted to be anywhere but there. Then Lorcan caught sight of Finny and he frowned. He did not seem pleased to see him there either.

Finny pointed to the spot where the opponent's body had been, and then at himself. 'Mind if I have a go?'

Lorcan threw his eyes to heaven, and again put on that false smile. He gestured for Finny to come on in.

Oh hell, yes. I may not beat you in a fight, you gurning idiot, Finny thought. *But I bet I can kick your ass at sport.*

Ayla followed King Nuada and his escorts down the citadel's long passages and out onto the gallery of towering sea caves. They were filled with the noise of the ocean. The gallery took them to a wide, swooping staircase, and they descended the many steps down to the sea. They turned their backs to the sea and the vermillion dusk and faced another cave mouth. This one yawned almost to the full height of the cliff – eight hundred metres. It was bathed in the burning red light of the sunset. Between the crashing of the waves, Ayla could hear a low hum. She felt it vibrating in her bones as they entered.

What is happening? I don't want to be here! Where is Finny? Oh, God, Finny, I wish you were here.

Ayla felt almost like she had just woken up. She could barely remember getting to the city.

Where am I? What have I been doing?

Her head pounded; her temples felt tight. Her body was walking, but she didn't feel as though she was making her legs do it.

She could remember Finny being meaner than he had ever been before. She remembered how jealous he was acting. Everything after that was in a haze.

He is so weak. This thought surprised her. *Why am I so angry? I feel like there is a hurricane in my head.*

They are all weak.

This is not me! Why do I feel like this?

They will all kneel.

No!

They will bow to the storm. Or I will tear them apart with wind and lightning.

Desperate thoughts swirled in Ayla's head. *Lann! Fergus! Taig! Please, help me! I need you so much! Oh, I wish we were all just back home in Kilnabracka! Why can't I just wake up and be home in bed? I will do anything for that again!*

They are dead.

No! Finny, Sean, Benvy! Where are you?

They will die also.

They are weak. You are strong. You are the Storm Weaver.

Please, Ayla thought, *hold on. You are Ayla. Don't let this consume you. Remember your friends. Remember your uncles. Remember who you are.*

They walked into the cave. Deep inside, where the evening could not reach, torches lined the walls and wavered with every swell of the ocean. The path was long, and tall antlered men and women stood along either side in procession, their eyes like hot coals in the shadows. As the hum became a melody, Ayla now realised the people were the source of the loud reverberating sound. Their singing sounded like a Byzantine choir of a strange and ancient race. When she passed them by they raised their hands in salute, each one scarred with a spiral on the palm. At last, Ayla and King Nuada and his aides came to another set of steps, and followed it down into a cavern. It was a garden of ore and crystal, illuminated by phosphorescent pools of purple and blue. At the other end was a waterfall.

'Here, my lady, we leave you,' said King Nuada.

The singing stopped, and soon Ayla was alone in the chamber. Not knowing quite what to do, she approached the falls. The white water cascaded down a series of shale outcrops, from a cavity up so high it was lost in the dark. The sound was soothing. The incandescence of the pools seemed to flare, and Ayla watched the water, feeling as if she had one foot in a dream. She struggled against the numbness that washed over her. She fought desperately to stay alert, not to lose all control over her mind. The flow of the falls began to change in almost imperceptible shifts, slowing and quickening, slowing and quickening. As the current faltered, something began to emerge in the movement of the water. Ayla took a few steps back and then could see. The cascade formed a face. It began to speak.

'YOU HAVE COME.'

Ayla didn't know what to say but found herself speaking almost involuntarily.

'I have.'

'I AM THE DAGDA, ALL-FATHER.'

'It … It is an honour to meet you, All-Father.'

This was not her speaking. *Ayla! Wake up!* She tried to command herself.

'LONG HAVE WE WAITED FOR YOU.'

'Tell me, please. How do I find Maeve?'

Inside Ayla's mind she tried to start a chant. *'I Am Ayla! I am Ayla! I must remember who I am.'*

The face in the waterfall paused for a moment.

'YOU HAVE FOUND HER ALREADY.'

'Daughter.'

From the shadows, a horrible wretch emerged. Her face was only half-formed, the left side of it a web of brambly roots. She was hunched and cloaked, and she lurched towards Ayla, extending a hand of twisted wood.

'I have missed you so,' the awful creature said.

The King on the Hill

Far away from the Danann sea caves, Benvy, Sean and Ida were preparing themselves for the next leg of their journey. It was Benvy who saw it first: a huge dog bounding over the crest of a nearby hill. Both she and Sean shrieked with fright, grabbing their weapons and diving to protect Ida. The beast was soon joined by another. They were as big as the wolves, but were clearly wolfhounds, though larger than any Sean and Benvy had ever seen. To their huge relief, Cathbad went out to face them. But the wolfhounds didn't attack him and it was clear their tails were wagging.

'Bran! Sceolan! Good to see you, old friends!'

One of the dogs had its enormous paws on Cathbad's shoulders, and matched the priest for height. He was licking the old man's face feverishly, while the other spun on the spot, impatiently awaiting his turn. What surprised Sean and Benvy most was to see Cathbad express so much affection for something. He called the group over.

'Children, this is Bran and Sceolan. They are friends, and will be our escorts on the road to Tara.'

The dogs trotted over and sniffed at the young travellers' feet and snuffled into their stomachs, nearly knocking them over. Ida was delighted, burying her face into their fur and laughing. The hounds didn't seem to mind.

'Gather your things and douse the fire. We should reach the Hall of Brú by nightfall.'

The dogs took turns to carry Ida on their backs, and even carried Benvy and Sean for a time. They lead the group over undulating countryside, through forests and over rivers. Occasionally, one or both of them would sprint off ahead to scout the way, or trot around the group in wide circles of patrol. The children had never felt safer.

Cathbad explained that they once belonged to a great warrior, but he had died and now the dogs were respected as warriors in their own right. They certainly were not pets.

'Although I think young Ida would like them to be,' the druid quipped.

By evening time the land had become flatter and swathed in lush forests. They passed a few simple dwellings, and on the rivers saw men and woman in odd round boats, fishing and hauling nets. Whoever they passed stopped to wave and pay particular respect to the dogs. The others, including Cathbad, they looked at with some suspicion.

Once again, the horizon was a vivid cherry-red as they arrived at a more concentrated group of round houses, their fires lit for the night, and the smell of cooking spilling from their windows. By now they were starving.

'Soon you will eat, I promise you. We are nearly there. Goll, give them some Arrowgrass and show them the incantation. They will need to understand our tongue now.'

The strange plant Cathbad called Arrowgrass tasted like aniseed and was very difficult to break down and swallow. Sean seemed to grasp the incantation part far easier than Benvy, and he began to speak in the old Gaelic language almost instantly, much to his friend's annoyance.

'Oh, look at the nerdlinger, able to speak a new language straight away. Must be all those hours you learned speaking Elvish and Klingon, Sheridan.'

Eventually, after a couple of recitations, Benvy could understand him. And when she spoke in English, she could hear it spill out of her – her voice, but different words.

Cathbad pointed ahead where the ground rose to a single high hill dominating the view. On top of the massive hill, fat bonfires burned at each compass point. Between the bonfires, on a bank of earth, a high wooden wall reached up into the night. There was one large gate.

'The Hill of Tara, the Hall of Brú,' declared the druid. 'Or you might have heard of it in your school books as the House of the High King.'

As they neared the hill they saw the great gate was opening, and a cluster of torches were spilling out. They were to have a welcoming party, and the thrum of hooves confirmed it. Before long, six men and six women, all atop proud chestnut horses, surrounded the new arrivals. The riders held long spears and wore metal caps that covered their faces down to their noses, with decorated holes for the eyes. The men's skin was tattooed with lumpy scars in the shape of spirals, which were painted red. The welcoming party bowed in their saddles and spoke with Cathbad. After a few words, the riders turned and lead Cathbad, Sean, Benvy, Goll and Ida up the hill and through the gates of the fort. Bran and Sceolan ran ahead.

Inside the walls many people came and went. Most were ferrying weapons from forges, and were laden with swords, bows, spears and armour. Blacksmiths clanged hammers on hot orange blades, creating nebulae of sparks from the

bellows. At the top of the stockade, along its entire cir-
cumference, guards stood in still sentry, facing out in all
directions. The house itself was uncomplicated. It was built
with large wooden planks, set with mud and wattle, with
a high conical roof of tight thatch. Smoke drifted into the
sky from its peak.

The troop dismounted, and their horses were lead
away by children who looked at Benvy, Sean and Ida
with unabashed curiosity. The group was escorted into
the building. It was warm and filled with the smell of
food. Wide corridors ran off to the right and left, but they
were brought straight ahead, through two heavy doors to
the main hall. In the middle was a huge fire pit, and the
smell of burning peat was everywhere. Around the fire,
tables were being set with metal plates and goblets, but
the people left as soon as the group entered. At the far
end, wooden steps ran up to a pair of thrones, upon which
sat a heavy, bearded man and a slender, fair woman. They
both wore silver crowns, delicately forged into the shape
of brambles with blackberries and all.

Cathbad bowed low. Goll bowed too, and tugged at the
friends to do the same.

'Rise,' the king commanded. 'There is no need for formalities with you, Cathbad.'

The old man got up.

'It is good to see you again, oh Brú and Étain.

Although, of course, I wish it were under other, better circumstances.'

'Indeed. It is bittersweet. You have changed quite a bit, old friend. I see that they wear odd clothing where you have been. But whatever your appearance, there are more important matters to discuss. You are here, of course, on account of the Daughter of Maeve.'

'I am.'

'Our spy has told us that the Lost Sister escaped her prison. This was not good news, of course. But when we learned the Daughter had also returned, we knew we had to prevent Mother and Daughter from meeting and joining forces. My spy was sent to retrieve the Daughter, but we fear the Danann have got to her first. The Blood Dusk is upon us. We have been preparing for the War. With the Daughter's return, a victory is even further from us. Who are your companions?'

'These, oh King, were two of the heroes selected by the Sons of Cormac to rescue the Daughter. Benvy, Sean, stand.'

The two friends did as they were bid. They stood and bowed. Ida hid behind Benvy.

'So the Sons of Cormac will succeed in sending the rescue at least. They would be saddened to know of how it is unfolding. And the third hero?'

'He is with the Daughter.'

Brú grumbled disapprovingly.

'Pray, then, that he has some influence over her.'

Queen Étain beside him spoke next.

'You are weary, children. We will remedy that.'

Her voice was smooth and soothing. She had a kind smile and deep-green eyes like bottle-ends.

'Yes, it has been a long road for you,' Brú agreed. 'When you have eaten and rested, we will talk. Now, to these other two. Goll, I know.'

'Hello, Uncle,' Goll said.

Benvy frowned. 'Uncle?' she asked, astonished.

But Goll just shrugged and smiled.

Brú provided the answer to her query: 'My sister's boy. A bag of trouble, if you ask me.' The king frowned at Goll, who bowed again sheepishly, and took his leave. Brú continued, 'And the little one?'

'That is Ida, your Highn… oh King … of Kings!' Sean blurted.

Brú looked nonplussed.

'I will have Cathbad explain,' he said as if tiring of them all. 'For now, you should rest.'

Two young wards emerged from a doorway, and Sean, Benvy and Ida were led to a room with a selection of fat straw mattresses. A small table held three plates of steaming food and leather gourds of water.

'Right, we need to talk about exactly what's happening

here, Sheridan,' declared Benvy. 'I have a lot of questions for this Brú character.'

'Yes, definitely,' Sean replied. 'But, mind if we eat first?'

'Absolutely. I'm *starving*.'

They had barely finished their plates, let alone talked, when each one lay back for a few minutes onto the mattresses and promptly fell into the deepest sleep of their lives.

The next morning Cathbad woke them at dawn. They were given a breakfast of bread and pork, which they devoured, and a few minutes to splash water in their faces and prepare for another audience with the High King.

'Be careful how you speak to him,' the old druid advised, looking at Sean in particular. 'Brú is a good man, but this is not the twenty-first century. He can be brutal, as can all the people here. They are born to hunt and fight. Death is a daily visitor. So mind your words!'

Then he added: 'You have achieved great things. So you have their respect – just don't abuse it.'

After they had washed, Benvy, Sean and Ida were given some new clothes: green tunics with a dark-brown belt, brown britches, leather sandals and hooded cloaks. The material was coarse, but their own clothes were filthy rags, and so to put on anything dry and fairly clean felt good. Sean and Benvy inspected each other's new look with great amusement.

'You look like a chubby Robin Hood,' Benvy said, sounding a bit more like her old self.

'That must make you Little John,' Sean shot back, happy to be able to banter with Benvy once more.

Ida was admiring her new clothes, running her hands on them. She had survived the whole time in a few rags and Sean's tattered hoody, and this was the first time she had proper clothes of her own.

'You look great,' Benvy said to her, smiling.

'Thank you,' Ida replied shyly.

Sean and Benvy gasped.

'Oh, my God! You spoke!'

Ida looked puzzled, and then ecstatic.

'Ha! I can! I can talk!'

The words were a little slurred, her tongue taking time to relearn its function.

'This is amazing!' Benvy felt like crying.

'So, where to start? Where are you from? How long were you down there? Oh, I forgot …' Benvy felt awkward. 'Cathbad said you can't remember?'

'No, I can't. Not really. I lived in the woods. I had a brother, a little one. There was a place we used to play, an old place. My father said it was where the *Shee* lived. Fairies. One day, we played there. I felt grabbed. And there was darkness. And then, then I remember you. In that terrible underground place. It frightened me so much there.'

'We will get you home, Ida. I promise,' Benvy assured her.

They found the whole of Tara was buzzing once again with activity, the reason for which was no longer ambiguous. Food was being placed in sacks, blades were sharpened, horses were armoured and everywhere men and women were preparing for battle. Even young children were taking spears from a rack or swords from a pile. All of this made Sean and Benvy very nervous.

The High King, Brú, was waiting for them in one of the stables. He was preparing his horse – a gigantic stallion, brilliant white with shining, intelligent eyes. Its flanks were scored with pink scars; it had evidently seen many battles. Sean and Benvy were surprised to find a king doing this for himself, but the man was taking great care in the task. He spoke to the horse as he worked, and the two clearly held a bond.

'This is Aonbar,' he said.

The horse, to the friends' astonishment, seemed almost to bow.

'He is a great warrior. I have never fought without him.'

'He's very beautiful,' Benvy said.

Pleased, Brú smiled.

'He is, child. Beautiful and fierce. So, now. It is time we talked. You slept well?'

'Like the dead,' said Sean, and added quickly, 'oh King.'

Brú turned to face them now. 'Then I am glad you

woke. Walk with me.'

They followed the High King back out into the open air to stroll among the bustling crowds.

'We are at war with the Danann!' he said. 'Tomorrow, on the plain of Muirthemne, either Man or Danann will be vanquished.

'For many ages, we were allies. When they arrived, we accepted them onto our land. We traded gifts: they gave us knowledge of magic; we gave them a home. But balance had always to be maintained. Neither was to take from the other more than what was offered. In that arrangement, we found peace and prospered.

'Our wisest men, the Council of Druids, known as the Old Ones, were the guardians of the Danann gift. They gave the rest of us men only what we needed, for fear that it would corrupt us, though they themselves grew power-ful. You are aware, I believe, of the tale of Maeve and her Danann lover, the Red Root King?'

Sean and Benvy nodded, and Brú continued: 'Man and Danann joined forces; the lovers were banished and their child sent to safety. We believed that both sides feared the Daughter's return. But now we know that was not the case. It seems the Danann corrupted one of the Sons of Cormac, Taig, and sent him to deliver the girl to her par-ents, the Red Root King and Maeve. In return, Taig was promised eternal life in their kingdom. It was the Danann who released Maeve from the prison. It was the Danann who restored all her power, and helped her to lure her daughter back into her arms.'

He stopped walking and turned to them.

'Your friend, Ayla, is the only offspring of a Danann and human union. In their hands she is the most powerful weapon in the world. They need her to ensure victory. And now they have her, I fear the war is lost to us already.'

There was a long silence, where the friends were unsure of whether they should speak.

Benvy couldn't keep quiet. 'But that means Ayla has gone to the enemy?'

'Yes.'

'And we are going to a battle with them? Tomorrow?'

'Yes.'

'And she will fight for *them*?'

'No, child. They will fight for her. *She* is the enemy now.'

Finny and Lorcan had been battling their own private war on the sportsfield. Finny was trying to get his breath back. The match had been going on now for almost an hour, and both of the boys were feeling the strain. They had jousted and parried and slapped and swung at each other, without holding back, each at times getting the upper hand, but the deadlock was stuck fast. Finny wiped blood from a painful cut on his arm. He hadn't been able to avoid the blow, but it had not stopped him winning the match.

No one in the crowd had ever seen the game played like this: lifting the ball with the weapon; weaving past the opponent; flicking the stone sphere in the air and smashing it through the hole from distance. They were cheering and laughing with disbelief. Lorcan was picking himself off the ground, wiping his bloody nose. He looked utterly ashamed at first, and Finny feared he might want to fight for real. But then that grin erupted across his face and he walked over to smack Finny on the back and laugh. For the first time, Finny didn't want to punch the smug smile off his face.

Then suddenly the crowd fell silent. The sky had darkened, kneading itself into a storm. Thunder drummed through the gathering clouds. The Danann had all turned to look in the direction of the caves.

Before Finny could crawl through their legs, he heard a sound, louder than the tempest. It was like the blast from a ferry, or a hundred ferries. Lorcan had grabbed his arm, and the look on his face was no longer happy. He was urgently trying to tell Finny something, pulling his arm and pointing to leave in the opposite direction. But he was ignored, and Finny pushed through the herd of Danann to see what had grabbed their attention.

The blast had come from the top of the cliff. It was a huge conch shell, the scale of which could only be appreciated by seeing how it dwarfed the Danann who had blown it. He was only a speck, and the shell was at least four times his height. It had announced the appearance of some people on the cliff-side gallery. They stood at the edge, minuscule compared to the sea caves behind them, and it was hard to make them out. The crowd came to life again, and all started moving towards the beach to get a better look.

Lorcan again tried to take Finny away; his voice was raised and he was obviously distressed. But Finny was too curious and followed the crowd onto the beach. Now at last he could see who had appeared. King Nuada was there, surrounded by a phalanx of guards, with the shape-changing woman, Nemain, just in front. Beside the king, Finny could see Ayla and what looked like a hunchback. The figure was hooded with a dirty grey cloak and clung to Ayla, practically hanging off her back. The crowd waited for one of them to speak. Finny assumed King Nuada would address them. He couldn't believe it when it was his friend who spoke.

King Nuada stepped aside, and Ayla moved towards the edge of the platform. The hunchback did not leave her side, and Finny could make out a gnarled hand holding on to his friend's elbow. Ayla raised her hands to silence the crowd.

'Danann!'

Somehow her voice carried to the beach, amplified by the caves. The people listened. Lorcan appeared at Finny's side and tried to haul him away, but Finny shrugged him off. He couldn't believe it! *How is this Ayla? What is she doing? Why are they all listening to her? Ayla! What have you done? What has happened to you?*

Ayla shouted something in their language.

The crowd erupted in a fierce, baying cheer with fists in the air. Ayla's eyes began to spark. Clouds formed from nothing just above her head, broiling and turning black. Thunder peeled from them, and two huge bolts of lightning blitzed not down, but out over the heads of the crowd and up into the angry sky. Ayla shouted something again, and the crowd responded with adoration and aggression in equal measure.

As the Danann milled around Finny, he didn't know where to run, or what to do. *Why was Ayla up there, doing this? Why was she talking about war? Who was that weird hunchback?* He was utterly confused.

Lorcan snapped him out of it. The young warrior spoke urgently, and although his lips moved, the words that came out didn't match them, just like King Nuada. His teeth were stained green.

'You come with me! I have to speak with you, before we go for Muirthemne!'

'What are you talking about? What's going on? How are you talking in English like the High King did?'

'I stole some of what he used. A trick my brother taught me. But we have to go quickly so I can explain! I know a place.'

Finny still didn't entirely trust Lorcan, but the young warrior gave him little choice. He brought Finny back up the escarpment to the narrow passage they had first come through. The weather was wild and cold.

'We can speak here,' Lorcan said.

'What's going on? What did Ayla say to them?' Finny asked.

'She said it is time for war.'

'What? Why is Ayla suddenly talking about war?'

'Because that is what we have to do now.'

'To fight who?'

'To fight Man. The Danann want to destroy them. They have a good chance now they have the Daughter of Maeve.'

'Wait, what? Ayla, my friend, is going to war with these … freaks … to destroy *Man*, ie mankind?'

'I do not know 'I-E'. But yes. She is with her mother now. The Danann's mission is complete, and they have the weapon that will win the war.'

'Her mother? Wait! That old hag hanging on to Ayla? That's *Maeve*? But ... Why isn't Ayla fighting her? She wanted to come here to *kill* Maeve!'

'No, my friend. Ayla was drawn here to *help* her, even if she did not know it.'

Finny suddenly realised something.

'You brought us here! You knew you were bringing us to Maeve!'

'Yes. But before you make mistake of throwing that punch, listen to me. I was taking you to Brú. He is my uncle, and the High King of Fal. A long time ago, Brú asked me ...' at this Lorcan looked around nervously before continuing, 'Brú asked me to make friends with the Danann, convince them I was on their side, that I would spy for them. Really, I was spying for Brú.'

'You ... You're a double-agent? Then why did you take us here? Right into Maeve's hands! Finny was beginning to panic.

'Nemain, King Nuada's captain, found us. She was the hawk. Some Danann can do things like that. They can shape-shift: transform into animals or birds.'

'Yes, I saw Nemain metamorphose into a hawk, just before we fought. So, let me get this straight, you weren't meant to take us here at all?' Finny asked.

'I had no choice but to act like I had been taking you here all along instead of taking you to Brú! I had to keep my cover, at all costs. Playing that game with you and their warrior was all part of my plan, to buy time, to stay close to their leaders and to try and think of a way to stop it all, but I can't. We are too late. She is lost.'

'No!' Finny shouted.

'I'm sorry. Now we must go to war with the Danann army. Pretend that we are on their side. And then we will find a time to strike.'

'Oh, really? How will we do that? You aren't a one-man army, Lorcan. I hate to disappoint you.'

'No! I am the knife. A knife is better than an army. A knife, at least, can get close.'

CHAPTER 11

The Leaves in the Hurricane

Half a day's journey south of the plains of Muirthemne, Sean Benvy, Goll and Ida were among the opposing army belonging to the High King, Brú, making their way to meet the Danann on the battle-field. The day of the great clash of forces had dawned some hours before but the bloody dawn lingered. The land was entirely bathed in it: the trees, hills and rivers all sodden with scarlet light as if soaked in wine. The countryside shook with the vibrations of marching feet and stamping hooves as an army, consisting of five thousand men, women and children, made its way north.

Sean, Benvy and Ida were in a cart, driven by Goll and drawn by two strong mares. They had thick leather jerkins to wear over their new clothes and helmets with a frontispiece designed to help protect their faces. Sean was forced to carry his glasses in his pocket and was struggling to see. He still had his hammer, and Benvy held her javelin in her lap. Even Ida had been given a stubby sword and a small round shield. Both Benvy and Sean were not sure if the magic of their weapons would work here, after the failure at the Pillars. They hadn't a clue what they were going to do if their weapons didn't come to their aid. Both felt sick with nerves.

Cathbad rode at the front, alongside King Brú and Queen Étain. She too had been transformed into a fierce-looking soldier, with a long sword on her back and a tall lance in her right hand. The royal pair sat side by side in a chariot, pulled by the mighty Aonbar. It was the only chariot drawn by just one horse. The hounds Bran and Sceolan trotted faithfully beside the High King and his queen. Behind, with waving spears and javelins, the army stretched on like the body of a vast and spiky millipede. Deep drums kept the march forward in time. Around the leading group, the rest of the men and women seemed determined and well-prepared; Sean realised it was probably not their first time to go to war. Some of the children,

however, seemed awkward in their armour and, every now and then, they missed the beat of the drum and struggled to keep their heavy lances upright. Benvy feared for their survival.

Sean and Benvy tried to talk to each other many times, but found that words had lost their place. This was a time for contemplating the fight ahead and for steeling yourself against the high potential for death, Cathbad had informed them earnestly. The helmets mostly hid both their wide darting eyes and they were grateful for that; neither wanted the other to know they were so very afraid.

The procession rumbled on over hills and rivers and through woods of copper beech and ash until the sun was at its zenith. They arrived at a steep bank of earth that stretched off in either direction like a seemingly endless grass wall. Brú raised a hand and shouts of 'Ho!' echoed along the procession, bringing the army to a halt. Ahead, Cathbad turned in his saddle and beckoned someone forward. Sean and Benvy were surprised when Goll urged their own cart to the front of the great army; they had been sure that it was someone more important that was called for. All four of their little group stood, bowed to Brú and Étain, and helped each other down from the cart. The High King stepped from his chariot, while Cathbad dismounted.

'Come,' the old druid said, and the four of them climbed

behind him to the top of the bank.

They stood on a grassy ridge, with only a metre or two before them until the ground fell away again. It swooped down in a vast plain of grass, flat for miles around, giving way eventually to hills and vales. In the distance it all faded into darkness; a curtain of night had fallen across the horizon and was creeping towards them, swallowing the landscape into its black cowls. Deep within, there were flashes of white; spindly threads of light whipped the ground, and the growl of thunder reached the ridge.

'Our enemy approaches,' said Brú, gravely.

'Friends, too,' Cathbad said, pointing out a group of horsemen that galloped across the plain, hunted by the gathering storm.

Sean fumbled with his glasses, pushing the helmet frantically off his head and squinting through the cracks of the broken lens. Surprising Benvy, he started to laugh.

'Could it be them? They are different. But … Yes! It is! It *is* them!' he shouted, hitting Benvy on the arm over and over. She scowled and went to hit him back, but then stared, disbelieving.

'It … can't …'

'You know, I wondered if this might happen! When Goll showed up, the thought crossed my mind, but … It was just silly! But it is them! Look!'

The riders were close enough to see now. There were

two men at the front. They wore robes like Goll and had long silver hair and beards that streamed in the wind. Behind them were two women, also with snow-coloured hair. It wasn't these figures that were familiar to Sean, but the ones following them.

On great war-horses were two huge men. One, the largest, had a mane of red hair; the other, jet black. When Benvy saw whom Sean was staring at she thought her heart and stomach were going to fuse. The riders climbed the bank, dismounted and with a word and a pat sent their horses down to join the throng. They all approached on foot, the four cloaked figures and the two giant men, and now there was no mistaking these two. Impossible as it was, Sean and Benvy could clearly see, despite being dressed in olive-green kilts and tattooed from torso to toe with spirals, that the two huge men really were Lann and Fergus. Lann was the most different, sporting a thick black beard. Taig was not among them.

It was the High King who bowed first, as the Old Ones approached slightly ahead of Lann and Fergus. Benvy and Sean thought it best to follow suit, but Cathbad remained standing, and addressed the Old Ones: 'Aed, Midir, my dear Earth-Brothers. Caer, Macha, my dear Earth-Sisters. I fear I return in sorrow.'

'Cathbad, Earth-Brother, we join you in your sorrow. And we are here to help you in any way we can,' one of the women replied.

'I see you have brought the Sons of Cormac,' Cathbad continued. 'Two of them, at least. Greetings to you, Lann of the Long Look.'

On hearing the mention of his name, Lann stepped forward and bowed.

'Great Cathbad, I am truly sorry for all our failings. It is a strange thing to be given a task, and to hear that you have failed in it before it has even transpired. We hope that our lives were some recompense, when the time came. I'm certain when Taig gets here, he will say the same. He follows, we are sure.'

It can't be them. It just can't be, Benvy thought. Then she spoke aloud without meaning to, 'I watched you die!' As soon as she said it, her cheeks burned with embarrassment.

Lann looked at the girl and replied, 'I hope it was an honourable death.'

'I'm sorry. I just …' Benvy couldn't think of what to say. *They look so different: younger and … wilder. They look dangerous. And they don't know about Taig yet. They think he is following them! Why doesn't Cathbad tell them?*

'And who are these young warriors?' Lann asked, now aware of the young people.

'This is Benvy Caddock and Sean Sheridan. They are the ones you selected to save the girl.' Cathbad brought the friends forward.

'Benvy and Sean, it is an honour.' Lann inclined his dark head towards them.

'You really don't know us at all?' Benvy asked. It was too much to get her head around. These men had taken them on a death-defying quest to save Ayla – they had been through so much together. But here and now, Benvy realised, they were not the 'Big Fellas' she knew from Kilnabracka. These men were warriors at the *very beginning* of a four-thousand-year mission. They had never met Ayla, or heard of Limerick or even Ireland! *Time travel,* she thought, *makes my head hurt. I can't even begin to wonder if anything we do here will affect our future.*

'No, lass,' replied the giant of a man. 'But I'm sure I will.'

Fergus stepped forward, towering over all but Cathbad. He bowed to them all.

'Well, this is all very strange and confusing. I think it's best to let the scrap begin. Nothing like a battle for humanity to clear the head!'

The red sky had darkened to violet and thunder split the air as they returned to the waiting army. King Brú addressed them. There was no long speech; the words were few and direct.

'Gather your arms! Run into the tempest headlong and quell it! For the future of our race! For *Fal*!'

The sound of the multitude roaring in response, bashing sword and spears to their shields in unison, rose into the air to clash with the wind; storm for storm, iron for thunder.

'Benvy.' Sean held his best friend's arm.

'Yeah.'

'Stick together no matter what.'

Then they rose to the top of the dyke and faced the armies of the Danann.

As the Danann army approached the battleground of Muirthemne, a gust of wind swooped around Finny like an ice-cold ghost, and the roof of coal-coloured clouds spat darts of lightning in searing flashes. He could see little through the sea of giant riders, the scene lit only sporadically by the lightning. He was sharing a horse with Lorcan. The mounts of the Danann were huge and the saddles so high that a fall would most certainly result in a broken limb. The warriors had broad backs and a strange, organic armour, like coral dipped in steel. Between the lightning flashes, they rode in darkness without formation, so he could see next to nothing of what lay ahead. All he could do was strain to get a glimpse of Ayla.

They were not far behind the leading party. Finny had seen them once or twice from higher ground on the long march from the Danann city. King Nuada, flanked by two important-looking soldiers, led the army on a mount that dwarfed even the others. His captains, Finny guessed. The shape-changer Nemain was likely to be one of them, given there were no antlers on either. Ayla was behind them, on a chariot pulled by four horses. The hag, Queen Maeve, hung off her back like a sack of bones. Ayla's arms were raised and even from this distance Finny could hear the deep chant that seemed to herd the storm overhead. When he turned to look around, the army covered the earth as far as he could see.

He had no plan in place to get closer to Ayla, and if Lorcan had one he hadn't shared it. His companion had said nothing for the entire journey and didn't look back to Finny once. Up close, Finny could see the spiral scars that covered Lorcan's skin in detail for the first time. They looked like they had been cut deep, and not all that long ago; some of them were still scabbing. He had lathered them in fresh red paint and his face too. He carried a vicious-looking spear: a short staff with a long wide blade that was barbed along the edges. He called it his 'Gae Bulga' and boasted that it would take on a life of its own on in the heat of the battle.

Finny still wasn't entirely sure who its target might be. *I wish to God this idiot would tell me what he intends to do. Are we really heading for a battle? I mean … It can't happen, can it? Those swords look real. Those spears. Holy God,* he thought, *we could die here today. But not if I can help it!*

Finny decided to focus on Ayla and how he might get

close and wrench that hag off her. *That witch must be controlling Ayla, somehow. I just need to find a way to break her hold.*

The procession stopped and the horses reared and stamped their enormous hooves. Everywhere he looked he saw the burning eyes of Danann – their mounts flaring up as a fresh barrage of thunder detonated above them. Where the canopy of storm clouds ended the sky was a deep blood-red – the colour of fresh meat. Finny stood on his saddle to try and see what lay ahead. King Nuada and his captains had drawn long swords from scabbards on their backs. Ayla's chanting was becoming more feverish, and the clouds overhead were beginning to broil. Finny's hair stood up and the fillings in his teeth hurt because the air was charged with so much electricity, and the storm was straining on the leash. Ahead of them was a wide, yawning plain of dark grass that rose to meet the distant silhouette of a vast army – standing, waiting. Finny could hear their chanting, and when that suddenly stopped there was a moment of silence. It was almost serene. Then the opposing army roared, and Finny watched them spill over the ridge like a pitiless and unstoppable tsunami. Around him the Danann warriors let out their war cries and moved as one to meet the enemy.

There was no time for Sean to be afraid, though his heart hurled itself against his chest machine-gun quick. His helmet hopped up and down on his nose as he ran and he could hardly make out anything around him. His breathing was so loud it drowned out the surrounding roaring voices, and he felt every shudder of his footsteps as they pounded the grass, trying desperately to keep him upright. In his left hand the hammer felt light, while in his right Ida's grip tightened and loosened and tightened again, and all he could think of was: *don't let go!* Benvy held Ida's other hand. Together they had decided they would risk everything to keep her safe. Now Sean prayed they lasted long enough to do that.

For a moment his helmet settled and he saw the swirling, fulminating clouds whip the earth with lightning and hundreds of pairs of eyes, all on fire, surging towards them. The Danann figures were inhuman – giants with burning crimson eyes and antlers arcing from their heads. Sean felt like they were facing the armies of hell. Everything was shaking, as if the whole earth was being rattled. It was not how he imagined battle, and it was nothing like in his books. There was no preparation, no plotting for survival, no game-plan. There was no stand-off with a single opponent while around him duelists clashed in choreographed swordplay. There was only turbulence and anarchy and a deafening sound. All he could do was keep going and pray.

As the two forces met in one huge shockwave, Sean felt something like a freight-train hit him on the shoulder and, before he knew it, he was face down in the grass and he could not get up.

Ida's grip was so tight that she fell with Sean when he was struck. Ida threw herself over him protectively – just as the assailant raised a spear to thrust through them both. Benvy was about to cast her javelin when a rock struck the Danann warrior between the eyes and he fell from his giant steed, swallowed by the frenzy. Goll had joined them. He hauled Ida to her feet, and quickly pushed some red leaves into Sean's mouth. Re-energised, the boy shot back to life as if emerging from underwater. All the while, Goll was frantically staving off attacks from every angle, firing stones from his hip, like bullets from a gunslinger. When Goll ran out of stones, he rubbed his hands together and clapped. Five Danann were pitched from their horses. More took their place, and it looked as if all four friends would be trampled into dust. But a huge man with a mass of red hair and a fiery beard – Fergus – rushed in to tackle one of the horses with his bare hands, putting his shoulder to its ribs and driving it into the others, riders and all. When they fell like dominoes, Fergus leapt upon them and the finish was violent and quick.

'Stick with me!' Fergus shouted over his shoulder, 'And crack a few heads – if ye can!'

On the other side of the battle, Finny was trying to stay close to Lorcan, but it was like trying to catch a balloon in a gale. Lorcan declared his treachery on the Danann as soon as the two sides clashed, swinging the vicious-looking spear into red-eyed warriors to his left and right, and then diving into the fray, with what Finny swore was a giggle. Finny himself was thrown from his horse and for a few hellish seconds was on the ground in a stampede, pounded and stamped and kicked, with blades stabbing the earth beside him and lifeless bodies landing loudly beside him in the grass.

The battle was riotous and violent, and Death was everywhere, clawing ravenously at Man and Danann with unbiased glee. Lorcan had been right about the 'Gae Bulga' spear too − Finny could see it spin and thrust and parry and hack, almost independently of its owner. Finny drew his own sword, and although the blue light shone brighter than before, he was too confused, and too afraid, to use it. There was no room to swing, only bustling violence that he did well to avoid. Finny tried his best to imagine himself in a match, just as he had at the loom all that time ago. For now, he weaved among the brutality, following the path carved through the fighting by Lorcan. Finny was heading for where the storm was at its most aggressive: a point not far ahead where there was a concentration of swirling, flashing thundercloud, stirred by Ayla, still in her chariot.

Except she was not in the chariot. As Finny got closer, he saw that Alya hovered above it, her entire body fused with electricity. For ten metres around her the ground was clear as crackling lightning pulsed through the air in a protective cage of light. The huddled form of Queen Maeve stood in front of her daughter, gazing up at her offspring with eyes like Catherine wheels, her scrawny arms raised to the tempest. Lorcan did not hesitate. He ran into the clearing. Finny followed, not really knowing what would happen next and what to do when it did.

Entering the clearing caused him instant pain. The shock ripped into Finny, his body convulsing against it, his blood carried on a network of pulsating, hot agony. He saw Lorcan smothered by current, screaming in distress. And then, among all this madness, the most incomprehensible sight of all: The Streak, his principal from St Augustin's, Fr Shanlon.

Fr Shanlon stood in the burning grass with eyes that glowed with a piercing starlight-blue. He was wrestling with the electricity that had engulfed Lorcan and wrenched it from him, squashing the lightning between his hands and extinguishing it. Then The Streak ran to

Finny, and did the same thing to him, hauling the blitzing fronds of lightning off the boy and stamping it out under his feet.

The pain left Finny instantly. *It really is true about The Streak! What Lann said really is true!* Finny thought as he stared at the priest in wonder. *He really is a druid. I still can't believe it.* But there was no time to understand it, because Finny saw that behind the priest Lorcan was on his feet again. The young warrior raised his fearsome spear – the Gae Bulga – ready to throw. Suddenly Finny realised, with horror, that he was not aiming it at Maeve – but at Ayla. Just then Lorcan threw the weapon.

Finny swung his sword up, faster than ever before. Its blue fire erupted along the blade, which lengthened to reach the Gae Bulga. Finny's sword caught the spear as it soared through the air, cutting it in half at the shaft. The barbed blade spun but its course was only slightly altered. It still met Ayla's right hand, slicing her at the wrist, but mercifully not removing the hand. A torrent of lightning erupted from Ayla's wound. She screamed from the cocoon of electricity in which she was now enveloped. Then she fell to the ground, senseless.

For the briefest moment the fighting around them subsided and a crack appeared in the clouds. The thunder, so deafening before, faded, and warriors from both sides stopped hacking at each other to stare into the clearing.

They all heard the cackle. The hag was laughing, the sound of it carried around the entire plain of Muirthemne by some dark wind. Maeve shrugged off her tattered cloak and revealed herself. She was barely human, a grotesque tangle of flesh and wood. The side of her face that held the remaining bit of skin was distorted into a sickly grin. Maeve pointed her hands to the ground and screamed out a horrid incantation. Her voice tore at their ears, amplified to an agonising pitch.

With the last word of Maeve's invocation, she wrenched her hands up. In an explosion of dirt, masses of roots ruptured the ground and spewed out, reaching out for all of them. Lorcan ran towards Ayla's body, diving through the encroaching tendrils of roots. Finny hacked at the roots that grasped at him, severing them in single swings, desperate to stop him. From the corner of his eye, Finny saw The Streak, joined now by four old people, facing off against Maeve. But all he cared about was getting to Ayla first.

Only two hundred metres away, across the maelstrom of the battle, Sean and Benvy were huddled around Ida, staying as close to Fergus and Goll as they could. When the black blanket of cloud thinned, just for a second, everything seemed to stop. For a moment everyone on the battlefield looked to the centre of the plain where the storm had been at its most aggressive, but where now a single beam of sun fell defiantly to the earth. They all heard the horrible noise that seemed almost like laughter. They all saw what looked like huge tendrils of wood spew from the ground and writhe like the arms of an octopus. But the break in the clouds was a sign. It was the men and women of Brú's army who roared with approval, and they who felt a renewed vigour in the fight. The sunlight's appearance let them know they were getting the upper hand over the Danann, and they fought against the enemy with new hope. Antlers were snapped, horses brought down, red eyes were extinguished. Fergus beat his chest and howled with approval. He dived back into the fray, driven by the scent of a victory against the odds.

'There!' he shouted, 'My brother! Lann!'

He was pointing downslope to where Lann, his brother with jet-black hair and flowing beard, was fighting against two Danann warriors. The warriors were dressed in more elaborate armour than the rest – a sign of their high-rank. One of them, a very tall woman, even taller than Lann, was raining down vicious blows upon the giant man, and he was struggling for the upper hand. Her compatriot, whose face was concealed by an elaborate mask under the brow of the helmet, held back and seemed almost hesitant. Lann was on his knees now and it did not look like he could survive another barrage.

Fergus howled with rage when he realised he could not reach his brother. Frantically, he tried to clear a path through the seething masses. His violent anger was terrifying. Sean had seen a hint of it once before, in the Norman keep. But now it was off the leash, and Sean was terrified.

Beside him, Goll was struck on the head and fell to the ground. A Danann, swinging a huge mace, turned his attention to Sean, Benvy and Ida. They had no defence against him, but before the antlered warrior could swing again – two enormous wolfhounds set upon him. Bran and Sceolan pinned the Danann warrior to the ground and tore at him mercilessly.

Sean, Benvy and Ida ran to Goll's side and helped him up. Looking out over the battlefield, they were able to follow Fergus's progress through the crowds as they saw bodies flying high into the air. Not too far ahead of Fergus, they could see Lann; he seemed defeated and looked to be moments from the killer blow. His opponent's helmet had been knocked off, revealing a woman, whose strange beauty was obvious even among the carnage. Her black hair tossed in the wind and her red eyes burned as she raised her sword above the stricken Lann, ready to bring it down on his neck. But the other high-ranking Danann, who had seemed so hesitant in all of this fighting, suddenly sprang to life and blocked the blade as it came down towards Lann.

The woman was incredulous at this defence of her enemy; she seemed to have a look of total confusion on her face. Then her expression changed and she responded to the treachery with fury. She was incredibly skilful with her sword, but the traitor matched her skill and knocked the blade from her hands. Weaponless, the woman decided on another tactic.

Neither Sean nor Benvy could believe what happened next: she morphed in an instant into a huge hawk, beating her wide wings and clawing at her opponent with huge, yellow talons. The hawk wrenched the helmet from the other warrior's head and blond hair spilled out into the wind. The huge bird flew up into the air, arced and swooped down like a feathered missile, talons reaching out for the killer blow.

Sean and Benvy saw straightaway that the Danann traitor was the missing MacCormac brother, Ayla's Uncle Taig. Taig, who had betrayed them, and who had given Ayla over to the Red Root King. Taig, who had made Benvy love him like her own uncle, only to have that love shattered by betrayal. And now, here he was caught in the act, dressed in the enemy's garb and fighting with them against his own brothers.

Benvy could see Taig was trying to defend his brother Lann against the female Danann warrior, now transformed into a fearsome hawk. But Benvy was so angry with him, she barely noticed herself raise the javelin. She acted on pure instinct, and threw the weapon with every ounce of strength she possessed. It shrieked like a banshee as it sliced the air and passed through the body of the hawk in a searing flash. But the body that fell to the earth was not that of a bird, but of a woman. Benvy, panting after the exertion of casting the javelin, could just make out Taig running to the dead woman's side, his face soaked with tears as he cradled her head in his lap. Even from this distance, Benvy could hear him shout: 'Nemain, my love!'

In the clearing around Ayla, Finny was also witness to great betrayal. *Lorcan is going to kill her! Not on my watch, you bastard!* He threw himself into Lorcan's side with everything he had. They tumbled to the ground, but Lorcan rounded upon Finny in a second, pounding him with his fists and screaming furious curses.

'*Amadán! Amadán! Amadán!*' Lorcan shouted over and over.

Around them roots spread and writhed, hoisting the hunched wretch, Maeve, into the air and surrounding her like a giant suit of armour.

Since they had arrived on the scene, the four cloaked

Old Ones had not moved as their age would suggest they should. Rather, they spun and danced on the air like humming birds – moulding balls of energy from thin air around them, hurling them at the vine-like roots that spread out from Maeve, shattering the roots to pieces. But wherever the Old Ones broke through a strand of grasping wood always more came. Eventually, the roots were winning by sheer numbers, engorging all within their reach. The tendrils bound Cathbad and the others in their knotted fingers, and squeezed their bodies to breaking point. Maeve's laugh was cold and grating.

'Old fools! Weak, wretched, miserly FOOLS!' she howled. 'You were only given a taste of the Danann power. I have feasted upon it! The Dagda has made me more powerful than you can dream of. Do you think I need my daughter now? Do you think I need these antlered animals? I will crush the lives of all of you forever. I will crush you to *nothing*! There will be no memory of you! There will only be gods! And I will be their queen!'

At this final cry, Ayla was wrenched into the air by a new eruption of roots that closed around her like a fist. Lorcan, too, was ripped from Finny and was also imprisoned in the roots, and though Finny swung and sliced as best he could he soon found himself overpowered. Before the tendrils enclosed him entirely, he saw the roots, like giant limbs, bring Ayla before Maeve and pull a thread of light from the young girl's chest. This was passed to the evil queen, who tugged on it hungrily. All the while, Maeve laughed and began to grow.

As she expanded, she fused with the tendrils of wood until she resembled a wicker man combined gruesomely with flesh. Maeve was now ten metres tall, with eyes and mouth exploding into flame.

Finny could not breathe. *Am I going to die?* he thought desperately. There was only one small gap that he could see through. Finny felt his thrashing heart begin to slow, and an eerie calm washed over him like cold water. As he watched what he thought might be his final sight, he took comfort somehow in that what he saw through the tiny opening was not Ayla dying, or Fr Shanlon crushed or Lorcan lifeless, but his friend, Sean appearing in the clearing. And even though he thought this was the end for Sean too, a small ember of pride still glowed in Finny when he saw his friend raise his hammer over his head with a naive but admirable stubbornness. As Finny's consciousness drifted towards heavy, permanent sleep, he watched Sean's hammer blow land, the ground shake and the roots disintegrate into flakes.

CHAPTER 12

The Homecoming

The ground rippled as if it were the surface of a millpond and a boulder had been cast into its centre. The roots that gripped the Old Ones, Ayla, Lorcan, Finny and Cathbad were shattered into thousands of pieces. Stunned, Maeve staggered on unsteady legs, nearly trampling the limp bodies of her victims.

Lann and Fergus rushed to haul the Old Ones to safety, while Sean sprinted to Finny. Goll hoisted Lorcan's body onto his shoulder and took him out of the clearing. At the edge of the unfolding scene, Benvy stood with Taig. She handed him the javelin and looked into his blue eyes that were filled with pain.

'My name is Benvy Caddock. You don't know me, but in another life, another future – you did. And you were a good man, I know it. You loved that Danann woman, right?'

'Yes,' he replied, his voice shaking with sadness.

'And you were prepared to betray everyone for her, even your brothers?'

'Yes.'

'I know you are hurting. But you can make things right. It's time to redeem yourself,' she said. 'And I want that back.' Benvy said, pointing to the javelin.

Then Benvy took Ida by the hand and they raced to Sean and Finny's side.

Taig lifted Benvy's javelin over his shoulder and turned to face the fearsome sight of Queen Maeve. 'I may never be forgiven for my treason. My betrayal will haunt me like a shadow. But at the least, I can do one thing for Fal. I can send this weapon through your chest, you twisted, miserable, cursed hag!'

He cast the weapon. It seared through the air and blew a hole through Maeve's chest. She stared down at the wound. Her face, now entirely made up of roots, twisted into a confused grimace and she dropped to her knees as the vines of her body withered, dried and cracked. With

the last flicker of fire from her eyes, a spark caught hold of her dessicated limbs, and the evil queen burst into roaring flames and collapsed completely.

A huge cheer rang out across the plain. Benvy and Sean were too busy with Finny to notice.

'Oh, God, he's dead! Finny's dead! What do I do? What do I do?' Sean cried out, overwhelmed with panic.

Gently, Ida pushed him aside. She took a tangle of yellow grass from one pocket and a handful of crushed purple flowers from another. Ida squeezed them together in her hands and pushed them into Finny's mouth, making him chew a little by moving his jaw. With a huge intake of breath, the boy jerked and woke.

'Ayla!' was the first word out of his mouth. Desperately he looked around, hardly registering that it was his long-lost friends that helped him up. A few metres away, bright red curls poked out from under a heap of clothes. He half-hobbled, half-ran to her, and Sean and Benvy followed.

'Here!' Ida handed him a fistful of the mulch, as Finny was moving towards Ayla.

Finny seemed to realise who Ida was then. It was the goblin-girl. 'What? You? How are you …?' But his priority was still Ayla. 'Please, help her,' he implored those around him.

Carefully they lifted Ayla's head into Finny's lap. She was frighteningly gaunt and pale. Finny put some of Ida's mixture into Ayla's mouth and worked her jaw for her.

But nothing happened.

'Oh, God, no,' Finny pleaded.

Benvy began to weep. Sean too. 'She's gone, Finny,' he said quietly.

'No! Please, give me more of that stuff!'

'That's ... That's all there is, I'm sorry. I'm so sorry.' Ida could do no more.

Sorrow and defeat settled on them all like a smothering cloak and, just then, a long-fingered hand rested on Finny's shoulder. It was Cathbad. He was sliced and bruised, and his breath came with a broken effort.

'Stand aside, Master Finnegan,' he said, assuming the tone of The Streak to get through to Finny.

The old druid knelt beside Ayla and began to sing. He opened his shirt and pulled a thread of light from his chest and placed it on hers. His eyes burned blue and then white as the colour flowed from his cheeks to hers. As Ayla's eyes flickered and then opened, pieces of him drifted away like flakes of ash on the breeze. He looked into Finny's eye and said: 'You're a good lad, Oscar Finnegan.'

And then the wind took him.

Ayla tried to sit up. She was utterly bewildered, looking like she had just woken from a coma.

'Where am I?' she asked.

'You're alive, that's the main thing.' Finny smiled through tears.

'But … What happened? Was there an accident? Who are all these people? Why is everything on fire?' She began to get scared and her voice was rising in panic. 'Uncle Fergus? Uncle Lann? Where are my uncles?'

Finny tried to calm her. 'Shh, Ayls. Just lie down for a minute. It'll be okay.'

The storm had dissipated, and the sun was carving the clouds apart. Around the clearing the groans of the wounded made for a sad chorus. But there were also cheers. A large shadow crossed them. It was Lann.

'Uncle Lann, thank God you're okay! Is everyone else okay? What's happened? A car crash or a bomb, or something?' Ayla still had no idea where she was or what had happened.

The three friends were shocked. It was obvious she really didn't remember anything at all. Finny held her close, and Sean and Benvy wrapped themselves around the two of them, and together they all tried to soothe her.

'The Danann are retreating, but the battle is not over yet,' Lann said. 'We have to finish them off.'

Finny couldn't understand a word, but Sean translated.

'I'll give you some Arrowgrass soon. It'll make you understand.'

'Ask him if he knows what has happened to Lorcan,' Finny said, with mixed feelings, 'The young guy, who was here with me?'

'He lives,' Lann said. 'I saw his brother, Goll, carry him away. But Lorcan will not fight again today. They will take him back to Tara, to heal. He and Goll are King Brú's nephews. Lorcan is much-loved. The Old Ones travel with them. They will take care of him there.'

Sean relayed this information, and Finny surprised himself by feeling relief at the news that Lorcan was alive. The young warrior had tried to kill Ayla in the end, but Finny understood that Lorcan had seen his actions as a last resort, a final attempt to save his people. Finny didn't like Lorcan one bit – in fact, he hated him – but he had a certain respect for him. Lorcan would do anything to protect his people. And if he had not cast that spear, Ayla would not have been stopped and everything would be lost. Finny's thoughts were interrupted as a breathless Goll arrived, calling out for Lann, 'Lann MacCormac! Grave news to follow the victory. King Nuada and the remaining Danann are escaping.'

'Yes, Goll. And we will hunt them down. I thought you were heading for Tara with your brother?'

'The Danann have my uncle and aunt, King Brú and Queen Étain! Bran and Sceolan are already in pursuit. We have to stop them! My brother is safe. I will go with you.'

They rushed to find horses and a cart, gathered the last remaining soldiers from the High King's army that were able still to ride and fight and set off in pursuit.

The cart jumped and jigged as Goll drove it at speed across the plain. Finny, Sean and Benvy did their best to absorb the shock for Ayla and keep her steady. Ida was using some of Goll's red leaves to suture the wound on her wrist, making a paste and applying it with expert care.

Around them, a throng of one hundred horsemen and women thundered through the grass, led by Lann, Fergus and Taig. The rest of the thousands of wounded had returned to Tara. In the distance, a group of Danann horsemen rode towards the horizon, where the last light was being washed with dusk.

They raced over hills at high speed and splashed through shallow creeks. Small trees were trampled as night fell and they moved in the dark. Bran and Sceolan returned and led the way, following the scent of Danann horses, frustrated at the slowness of the pursuit, although the hunting party did not rest and rode with ever greater speed as the dawn sun ascended to noon.

By late afternoon they had gained ground; they noticed blood had splashed the trail and knew the enemy was wounded and slowing down. As afternoon waned to evening, they reached the marshes and saw their quarry crossing the muddy bog. Up ahead, swathed in mist, great stone towers loomed.

'The Pillars!' Sean shouted. 'They're headed for The Pillars of the Danann!'

The cart was abandoned, useless in the wetlands, and Ayla was placed on Lann's horse in front of him. The others were put on the backs of horses too. Bran and Sceolan howled with delight, sensing the rewards at the end of a long hunt, especially now that their prey was hampered by the bog and grievous wounds. By the time the High King's men reached the end of the marsh, the Danann had stopped at the foot of the colossal pillars and were waiting.

Fergus laughed. 'So they're up for a fight! Excellent!' he shouted gleefully.

As the hunting party approached, Lann raised a hand and they came to a stop.

Up the hill, in the shadow of the stone towers, King Nuada stood behind the kneeling bodies of Brú and Étain. His soldiers held blades to the royal couple's necks. The Danann king's eyes flared red, and he smiled.

'Do not approach, Lann of the Long Look. Throats will be opened,' King Nuada threatened.

'You are defeated, Nuada! Return our king and queen to us and then, by all means, leave Fal by the same way you came. Afterwards, we will knock down every pillar so that you can never return.'

'Oh, we *are* leaving here, Lann MacCormac, never fear. And we don't intend to return. You have taken our *home* from us. You have taken our *future* from us. And so now …' He smiled. 'Now we are going to take your future from you.'

Brú and Étain were kicked and rolled down the hill towards them. As men rushed to help the couple, Nuada and the Danann riders disappeared into the mist and were lost among the Pillars.

'Eh. What did he mean there?' Sean asked, already suspecting the answer.

Lann turned to look at him, Benvy and Finny. Finally, he glanced down at the sleeping girl in his arms.

'It looks like we are taking you home, lass.'

Mary Sheridan had invited Podge Boylan back to her house, where, despite his protests, she insisted on calling the guards to tell them about what she had seen.

'Believe me,' the old man warned, 'they'll just think you're mad!'

Sean's father, Jim, was deeply concerned. 'Mary, love. This is crazy. Glowing stones and priests with lightbulb eyes! It's nearly midnight. You need to rest! The guards are on the case!'

'The guards will be on that priest's case now too, Jim. He knows what's going on. And I know what I saw!'

Podge has taken a seat at the kitchen table and helped himself to an apple. He bit into it with a loud crunch.

'The guards can do nothing,' he crowed, spitting flecks

of apple over the table, 'The war is coming! Eh, have ye any whiskey, by any chance? I could do with a stiff drink.'

'Remind me, Mary,' hissed Jim Sheridan, 'why you invited Podge-bloody-Boylan back to our house?'

'Because, Jim, he knows more about what's going on than all of us. And no, we have no whiskey, Podge. And will you turn down that radio, for God's sake, I'm trying to make a phone call!'

Podge instead, infuriatingly, turned it up. It was the news.

'We can neither confirm nor deny the reports. All we can say is that we are investigating and will get to the bottom of it. My own personal view is that it's some kind of prank or maybe some American TV show filming or something.'

'But Inspector,' the reporter pressed, *'we have reports of these strange happenings coming in from different visitor attractions in all parts of the country: Newgrange, the Ailwee Caves, The Poulnabrone Dolmen, The Rock of Cashel, so surely that negates the theory of the television show. Especially as there are no film crews in sight? None of the county councils seem to know of any filming.'*

'Look, we will investigate with due process. That's all for now.'

The old man clicked the radio off.

'I told ye. 'Tis-a-comin'!'

Mary had finally managed to get an answer at the Garda station.

'Hello? Yes, it's Mary Sheridan here. Garda Kelly is looking into my son's disappearance? Yes, I'm sure he is busy.
Yes, I have heard the news. It's to do with that. I think my
missing son might be involved. Please, can you ask Garda
Kelly to come to my house as soon as he can? Or any
guard. Quickly, please. Thank you.'

Garda Pat Kelly was pursuing his own line of inquiry.
Having had no luck at the MacCormacs' house, he had
decided to check out the site they had been working
on, up at the old Sheedy farmhouse. It was late, eleven at
night, but he couldn't head home before having a look. It
would keep him awake all night. He left the headlights on
and took a powerful torch from the boot. He thought for
a moment and took the baton and pepper spray too, as a
precaution.

He took note of the crushed jeep under the fallen scaffolding, and was preparing to take a picture, when he heard
a noise coming from the other side of the house. On his
way around, he tried to radio in, but all he could get was
static. Undeterred, he moved towards the sound, readying
the spray and pointing the torch beam ahead. When he
reached the garden, the noise was louder and there was
movement in a big mound in the far corner.

'Garda Inspector! Whoever's there, come out and take it easy now! I'll spray you if there's any bother!'

He squinted and rubbed his eyes with the back of his hand when he saw the stones in the mound begin to glow, and then vibrate.

'What in God's name ...'

The rocks split asunder, and a gaping hole widened on the side of the mound. Mist spilled out. It rolled away, and a figure emerged. He was huge – three times the height of a normal man. The creature, for that is what it was, had glowing red eyes and, strangest of all, long barbed antlers.

ALSO FROM MATT GRIFFIN

Magic exists beneath our feet, if we only know where to look ...

Growing up in a New York orphanage,
Ayla has no idea she has Irish roots. It is not
until she comes to Ireland that she finds out
just how deep her roots really are...